PRAISE FOR MICHELE ISRAEL HARPER

"*The Lost Slipper* is a retelling of two fairy tales that could have easily been enough to carry the story on their own, but the addition of 'Diamonds and Toads' to the Cinderella narrative brilliantly escalates the tension and increases our poor heroine's suffering. A thrilling, emotional tale for anyone who ever thought, 'Cinderella had it too easy.'"
—C.O. Bonham, author of *Runaway Lyrics*

"*The Lost Slipper* is a short but satisfying read about grace and kindness when beset with cruelty, creatively combining two beloved fairy tales into a new, complex fable."
—H.L. Burke, award-winning and bestselling author of over twenty eclectic fantasy novels

"As someone who enjoys every Cinderella iteration I've ever come across, *The Lost Slipper* blends my favorite familiar elements of the story with unique twists—such as who the Fairy Godmother really is and the behavior of the stepsisters. With allusions that bring to mind *Ever After*, *Ella Enchanted*, and *Into the Woods*, readers will enjoy how Harper weaves this story and will be left wanting more!"
—Alicia Grumley, poet, Cinderella aficionado, and cohostess of Diversity Is Lit Book Club

THE LOST SLIPPER

THE LOST SLIPPER

MICHELE ISRAEL HARPER

Love2ReadLove2Write Publishing, LLC

Indianapolis, Indiana

ALSO BY MICHELE ISRAEL HARPER

Wisdom & Folly Sisters:
The Complete Story

Candace Marshall Chronicles:
Ghostly Vendetta
Zombie Takeover
(Coming Soon)
Vampire Feud
Mummy Resurrection

Beast Hunters Series:
Beast Hunter: A Prequel Novella
The Lost Slipper: Cosette's Story

Kill the Beast
Silence the Siren
(Coming Soon)
Quell the Nightingale
Slay the Wolf
Stop the Snow Queen
End the Fey

Coming Soon:

Standalones:
Queen of the Moon

Dreamworld

Stars Collide

The Ravens

Altered Time Saga:

The Lady Bodyguard

The Lady Spy

The Lady Assassin

Altered Time Novellas:

Lady in Hiding

Making of a Lady

Lady Out of Time

Tales of the Cousin Kingdoms:

Ruby Dragon Kingdom

Diamond Unicorn Kingdom

Sapphire Griffin Kingdom

Emerald Pegasus Kingdom

Time of the Dragons

To all the girls in an impossible situation

*May you always be kind, have courage, and
create a beautiful story for yourself*

1

A BALL ANNOUNCED

*B*ack aching, Cosette took a moment from scrubbing floors to twist and stretch a few kinks out, then gazed around her in satisfaction.

They might not have any servants left to do the work, but far be it from her to leave anything half done. Or to live in a filthy home.

Giggling reached her ears a moment before her stepsisters, Anastasie and Drucelle, burst through the kitchen door, squealing and swatting at each other with goose-down pillows.

Cosette could only watch in horror as the pillows trailed feathers everywhere she'd just scrubbed. She raised up on her knees and yelled, "Stop!"

The girls froze, blinking owlishly at her, then at the mess.

Anastasie's dark curls were piled atop her head, tied in place with a kerchief, and Drucelle's straight-as-a-board flaxen shoulder-length hair was already wisping out of hers.

"Oh, by all the saints, désolé, sister dear," Stasie started, but was interrupted as Druce shot her a disgusted look and said to Cosette in a snooty voice, "Well don't just sit there gaping, dimwit. Help us clean this up before Maman sees!"

Cosette propped her fits on her hips. "I've spent all morning scrubbing this. You made the mess; you clean it up."

Unlike her other sisters, her real sisters, now married and off living with their new husbands, who could be prodded into doing their part, Cosette's stepsisters got that look on their faces—one that spelled trouble for Cosette.

"Who's to say you're not the one who made this mess in the first place?" Druce sneered.

"Honestly," Stasie put in, looking cross, "if the floor wasn't all wet, these feathers wouldn't stick to it so horribly."

"So clearly it's your fault . . ."

"And you're the one who needs to clean it up."

Both girls crossed their arms and glared at her, daring her to say otherwise.

Cosette thought about it, she really did. She had years of experience mothering her older siblings, and although every one of them was a terror, not one of them had the cruel streak these girls shared.

Most likely passed down from their mother.

Her eyes drifted to the stairs, where her stepmère, Comtesse Béatrice Reynard, now that she had married Cosette's père, kept the habits of nobles from pre-curse-era France and slept well past noon.

Cosette was often done with most of her chores by the time the woman crawled out of bed and started demanding things.

"Go on. Tell her. I dare you." Druce's eyes flashed, promising she'd play her role of wounded stepsister and happily see what punishments her mère could dream up today.

Cosette sighed. "At least help me. She'll wake any moment, and you know most days she punishes all of us."

Stasie swallowed, hard, but Druce just looked angrier, her hands balling into fists.

"Well then," Druce said. "I'll make *sure* to tell her you

were the one who wasted all this lovely down. When you should've been working."

Cosette shook her head and surveyed the room, trying to come up with a plan to clean up and conserve the feathers in the quickest way possible.

"Come on, Druce," Stasie put in. "Let's just get this all picked up before Maman sees, non?"

"Or . . ."

Cosette's head came up at their prolonged silence.

Drucelle had a wicked gleam in her eye, and she hefted the pillow that had been brought in from freshening outdoors. A few more feathers drifted to the floor and stuck.

"I do this!" Druce slammed the pillow into her sister's face, and Stasie shrieked and returned fire.

Cosette shushed them — "Girls, please!" — to no avail.

Her stepsisters raced upstairs, leaving down hovering gently to the floor in their wake, and slammed their bedroom door.

A bell started ringing in the kitchen.

Just as a knock came at the door.

Cosette raised her eyes to the ceiling, praying Saint Margaret would give her patience. "Can't I just move back in with my family? Please?"

But no answer came, and there was no family home to move back to.

Père had lost it again. Gambling.

Cosette climbed wearily to her feet and trudged to the front door.

As soon as Rosette, her sister, her best friend, had started secretly providing for the family, sending them what she earned from her hunts, their père had moved back into their family's country estate.

From there he'd made connections, married off his five eldest daughters, set up his sons in apprenticeships — though Cosette suspected Rose had more to do with that than their père—and then to top it all off, had married a wealthy aristocratic widow and had once again moved, this time into her château.

Just in time, too.

Cosette doubted anyone but she (and perhaps, her brothers) knew why the move had been so hastily done.

And now that Père had gotten what he wanted—a higher nobility title in his family tree—he spent his time looking for new business acquisitions.

And often losing them right after he'd attained them.

Her eyes glided over the wide foyer, marble floors and pillars, and sweeping staircase. This place would've been glorious, had they been able to maintain it.

Chips and cracks marred every surface, and the windows were boarded against looters. The only viable currency in the country right now was food, and it was all they could do to get it.

Those they hired to fetch provisions from the Mesdemoiselles' food wagon often disappeared, whether from wolves or weather or keeping the food for themselves, Cosette never knew.

So she scrubbed. And cleaned. And tried to distract herself from the gnawing hunger, and at first, to help her stepsisters see they didn't need to give up, to succumb to the hopelessness of the curse.

Now she had to tell herself that daily.

Life hadn't at all turned out as she'd expected.

If they couldn't find the wagon, they'd run out of food. And if they ran out of food, their squabbles would grow even more intense, angry. Cruel.

And if the cruelty reached higher levels—

The knock came again.

Cosette startled, mortified that she'd just been standing there, staring at nothing, lost in her worries.

She popped out the wooden brace across the door and jerked it open harder than she meant to.

A fist came flying at her face.

She ducked the blow, and a young man dressed in ruffled sleeves, powdered wig, and finery from days gone by stumbled past her. She raised the wooden door brace in case the young Monsieur had come to rob them, but non. He looked just as startled as she.

She quickly lowered her makeshift club and set it aside.

With a valiant effort and a rather acrobatic series of steps, he just barely kept from face-planting at her feet.

"Oh! Are you all right, Monsieur?" Cosette asked, her heart pounding from nearly being struck in the face.

She hauled him upright and dusted him off, even though he didn't need it. But she had to do *something* with her hands.

The young man pulled away as if incensed that she'd touched him, then took a moment to straighten his shimmery tan jacket, fuss with his lacy sleeves, and regain his composure.

Cosette's eyes riveted on his wig, and she bit her lip. It was askew, but she wasn't sure she could tell him.

Not out of spite. If she opened her mouth right now, she'd burst into laughter. Partly from nerves, and partly from seeing someone who cared about such things as finery show up at her door.

She tried not to think of the disaster behind her.

When she'd gathered enough self-control, she asked, "May I help you, Monsieur?"

"Ahem. My pardon. I—" His eyes riveted on her feet. Her bare feet.

It took all her strength not to tuck one foot behind the other. She slipped off her bothersome shoes every chance she got—it was simply so delicious to feel the cool marble or silky dirt or soft grass against her toes, she couldn't resist.

Just one more thing to be ridiculed for by her stepsisters.

Cosette wanted to hide, but she'd already tucked her skirts up to keep the fabric from dragging on the damp floor, exposing her ankles and her toes for all the world to see.

Then his gaze settled on a feather by her foot, and he took in the rest of the room.

Feathers everywhere, boarded windows, cracked marble—Cosette hustled him outside before he could see worse than feathers in the dim light, humiliated yet fiercely protective of her home.

Not her home. The Comtesse's home. That she spent all her time cleaning.

She lifted her chin and spoke in a sweet yet firm voice, hoping to distract him. "May I ask why you have come, Monsieur? Have the Mesdemoiselles' wagons been found, perhaps?"

He sniffed. "As if I would have anything to do with such witchcraft. Message for Comtesse Reynard, Mademoiselle."

The messenger slipped a heavy square of paper from his satchel and held it out to Cosette, nose stuck in the air, a look of disgust on his face for the state of the house and the peasant he was forced to converse with.

If only he knew.

Cosette dipped a curtsey and took it reverently. "Merci beaucoup, Monsieur."

He started to speak again, but Cosette's eyes were riveted on the thick, expensive paper in her hands, gilded in gold. It looked just like the invitations her mère, her real mère, received in a steady stream when they lived in Paris and everyone wanted her presence at their fêtes.

Cosette shut the door in his face without meaning to, entranced, her attention elsewhere, his voice a faint buzz in the background.

Excitement filled her. Might there be a reprieve from the drudgery her life had become?

The servant's bell rattled again. And again.

Cosette didn't even mind as the ringing grew more insistent. She hurried up the stairs to see what her stepmère wanted, hoping the invitation would be enough to pull her into a good mood after being awakened by her shrieking twins.

2

A BALL DENIED

"A ball. In Monsieur Gautier's honor." Stasie sighed, leaning on her broom and staring dreamily at a future playing itself out in her mind.

Quite possibly her future. On his arm.

Cosette smirked, her broom dancing around the room, doing more to clear the dried and half-stuck feathers than her stepsisters' brooms ever did.

The Comtesse was pleased with the invitation.

She was less pleased when she saw the state of the room downstairs. All three girls were immediately dispatched to clean it or not be allowed to attend, but of course, Cosette was doing the bulk of the work.

No matter. She enjoyed being with her stepsisters when they were in good spirits.

And were they in good spirits. They'd been talking about the invitation, the fête, and Monsieur Gautier since Madame Béatrice had read the invitation aloud.

One line especially warmed Cosette's heart.

Every peasant, servant, laborer, steward, and noble is heartily invited to attend and partake of the grand feast that awaits. Come one, come all.

Still, as kind as those words were, Rosette had warned her about him, and often.

"Isn't he so handsome?" Druce grinned at her sister, her entire face melting into a giddy expression. "They say he's been hinting at choosing a bride at each of the fêtes he's been throwing across the country. Can you imagine if it happens at our ball?"

"Ooh, I wonder who he's going to choose!" Stasie all but shrieked.

"Well if he's smart, it will most certainly be one of us."

The girls dissolved into giggles, leaning against each other to stay upright.

Cosette shook her head and spoke her mind. She'd heard plenty about this Gautier, most from Rose herself. "Monsieur Gautier DuBois is full of himself and a tease, never mind you thinking of marrying him. He's been angling for the throne since the royal family disappeared, and this visit is nothing more than gaining support for his bid for the throne. Not to mention others say there is something so . . . untrustworthy . . . about him. I mean, honestly! You'd do better with a dishrag."

Her stepsisters' mirth evaporated. Cosette froze.

She spun on them with wide eyes. "Désolé. Forgive me. I did not mean —"

Stasie looked hurt. "Of course you meant it. You meant it, or you wouldn't have said it."

"And what do you know of it, peasant girl?" Druce sneered. "He's more noble than you'll ever be. How can you begin to guess what he's like?"

Cosette bit her lip and didn't point out that she was of the noble class herself, and wealthy once besides, before her père's ships sank and her family lost everything. And even though her stepfamily would've outranked her in the France of before, not many still cared about such things.

They cared about surviving.

"I just meant—" Cosette said feebly. How could she have forgotten to whom she was speaking? She could say what she thought to her sisters, not these cruel girls.

"We know what you meant." Druce's eyes flashed. "And what would it matter if he was trying for the throne? It's not like we've had any leadership since the king and queen disappeared."

Fair point. Besides, the argument that choosing royalty outside French royal lineage just wasn't *done* seemed like a waste of words. Who cared anymore how things had once been done?

Cosette tried to apologize once more, but Druce cut her off.

"Besides, you won't be going, so it doesn't matter."

Cosette's mouth fell open. "Of course I'll be going! He invited all of us. I work just as hard if not more than the rest of you." She clenched her jaw. "I'm going."

Druce got that cruel look in her eyes that rivaled her mère's. "You step one foot outside this house tomorrow, and I'll tell Maman who really spilled the last of the milk."

Tears jumped to Cosette's eyes. "That was you!"

And spilling the milk could be a death sentence to a family who didn't know when their next meal would come rumbling through on a rickety old wagon.

Especially if they missed it again, as they had the last two deliveries.

Besides, Madame Béatrice assumed the cow had kicked it over, and Cosette had been careful not to say otherwise.

She'd never been able to spin a falsehood, not in her entire life.

Druce just raised an eyebrow. "Whom do you think she'll believe? You? Or me?"

Cosette wanted to scratch that haughty look right off her face. And honestly? It could go so many ways. Madame Béatrice could punish them both, just Cosette, Stasie for standing there and letting it happen, or Druce alone to make her hate Cosette even more.

They never knew what the volatile Comtesse would do.

Druce came close and got right in Cosette's face. "Tell me you won't go to the ball. Promise me."

Cosette stood perfectly still, afraid to move.

"I want to hear you say the words."

She couldn't say the words. If she said the words, she'd have to keep them.

"Druce, come now. What is the harm—" Stasie rarely got the chance to be nice, but if she attempted it, it was swiftly stamped out.

"The *harm* is our nobody little stepsister at *our* party, batting her lashes and trying to snatch our prince right out from under us. Can you imagine?" Druce barked a cruel laugh. "We'll be the laughingstock of the countryside!"

"You know he's not really a prince, righ—" Cosette bit her lip. How she missed the camaraderie of home, where they'd fought and tussled and bickered, but anyone could say what they liked and no one sought to purposefully wound each other.

And heaven help anyone outside the family who said something against them.

Stasie turned wide eyes on her. "Oh, but he could be! If the crown prince isn't found, he could very well be the next—"

"Silence, you fool!" Druce seethed. "Do you want to give her *more* ideas?"

Cosette threw her hands in the air, palms up, letting her broom clatter to the floor. "I have no designs on Monsieur Gautier whatsoever!"

Druce gave her a cold look. "That's Monsieur DuBois to you, peasant. So what will it be? Spilled milk? Or a ball where you don't belong?"

Cosette bit her lip.

"That's what I thought." Druce gave her a triumphant look before she spun away.

She hesitated next to where Cosette's broom had fallen, then threw hers atop it. Then she yanked the broom from Stasie's hands and added it to the pile.

With a start, her eyes riveted on the pan of feathers they'd spent the afternoon swiping from every surface in the foyer and on the staircase.

Cosette lunged, but she wasn't fast enough.

Druce heaved the dustpan, and feathers flew in an arc out into the room. A few floated, but most were sad, crumpled things that fell heavily to the ground.

Cosette gave a startled cry, but Druce shot Cosette a triumphant look and marched away, hand clamped around Stasie's arm.

Stasie's parting look was shocked, then sad, but it didn't leak hope into Cosette's heart this time. What good was she, what good was Stase, if neither of them was brave enough to stand up for themselves or each other?

3

TO FIND A SISTER

*O*nce a measure of calm returned, Cosette cleaned up the feathers, tossed them into the trash heap, as they were now unsalvageable, and set about making something for dinner out of nothing.

They may have relied on the Mesdemoiselles of the Mountain's wagons, but the three women had the only growing garden in France. They needed that food.

They were running dangerously low.

Besides, there were rumors the great huntress had defeated them. But if that were the case, who was now providing France with food? Or was that why it had been so long since they'd last found the wagon?

All things she didn't know, things that wouldn't matter if she couldn't barter with someone who *had* been able to find the wagon. She would have to ransack the servant's quarters again to see if there was anything left worth trading.

As she cleaned, as she cooked, she thought of everything she could've said—should've said—to defend herself.

According to the invitation, all were invited—Madame Béatrice had even said she couldn't go unless the feathers were cleaned up, implying she could, in fact, attend—and the petty jealousies of Druce were not going to keep her away.

After making four sad little quiches, vegetables wilted and hard to find among mostly flour for filler and the few eggs the hens still laid, Cosette set them out to cool.

She started to head upstairs, then paused, turning to look at the cooling food.

Something told her that if she wanted it, she should eat hers now. Not that she didn't trust her stepfamily, but, well, perhaps she didn't. Especially after today.

She stood there, clutching the rail, almost frozen with indecision.

The girls had been amiable enough at first, perfectly willing to gossip and chat and share ribbons, but as things got harder, the more they bickered, and the more they made cruel choices.

And her stepmère . . .

Cosette bit her lip.

At first, she'd been solicitous. Agreeable, even. Welcoming Cosette into her home, treating her generously, if not warmly.

But that had begun to change the longer Cosette's père stayed away.

Cosette would be working with her stepsisters, doing the chores of the servants, and she'd feel someone watching her. She'd turn to find cold, hard eyes directed at her, seething with something like . . . spite.

The expression was always swiftly, carefully wiped away, leaving behind a neutral expression, making Cosette question if she'd even seen it.

But then the explosions of anger came. The punishments. Pitting them against each other.

At first she searched her stepsister's faces, their reactions, to see if this was normal. If this was a side of her stepmère she'd simply never before seen, something she kept carefully hidden away from the world.

But she could never tell. Could never figure out *why*.

Stasie would freeze, eyes wide, maybe a little blank, and instantly try to make everything better if she could. Once the danger had passed.

Druce seethed with anger whenever her mother wasn't around, being just as cruel if not more so. Cosette thought the anger covered deep hurt, but Druce never let her close enough to the wound to help heal it. So it festered, and her stepsister grew increasingly bitter and bad-tempered.

And Cosette didn't know what to do. How to make it better.

If only her père would come home! Care for the family he'd taken on after getting rid of his first family.

All except her.

If only he'd left her behind as well.

Her père's words, as he'd kissed her goodbye, rang in her head. "Be good and don't cause a fuss. Listen to your step-mère, stay here, and above all, make your stepsisters feel welcome in our new home, eh?"

Which was just ridiculous. *They* should be welcoming *her* since it was their home, but of course she'd never say that.

And of course he wasn't satisfied until he'd heard her whisper "I promise."

She'd felt the words bind her as if shackles had been clamped around her wrists.

She'd always kept her word—it was the right thing to do, after all—but this felt different. As if her promise, once given, couldn't be taken back.

He'd winked, pinched her cheek—which she'd always hated, but she held in her wince for his sake—and he'd walked out that door. And she hadn't seen him since.

Why marry the Comtesse if he wanted nothing to do with her? Besides the higher nobility title. But he wouldn't have married her for that reason alone, could he have?

Even her père couldn't be that manipulative. That scheming. Could he?

Thinking about it all made her head spin.

And as if his words—and hers—had been shackles, she hadn't been able to shake them. No matter how many times she'd dreamed of running away, she hadn't been able to make herself do so.

A part of her feared the words held some kind of sway over her, but that was also ridiculous. She knew the truth.

She was a coward. Just like her père.

A pang lit Cosette's heart. She wasn't being fair to him, she knew that, but after marrying off her sisters, setting her brothers up in apprenticeships, and sending Rosette away—he'd certainly been eager enough to marry the Comtesse and move away from his grown children as quickly as possible.

And Rose . . .

Cosette almost burst into tears right then.

She'd do anything to see her sister again. Let Rosette know what had happened to her.

To perhaps . . . live with her?

She couldn't put her finger on what exactly was wrong here, what was broken, what caused the vicious reactions of her stepmère and stepsisters, but she needed out. She'd beg, she'd plead, she'd work her fingers to the bone—anything to convince her favorite sister to let her come live with her.

Whatever sparse, remote hunting cabin Rosette currently haunted between hunts had to be better than this.

Cosette blinked away the daydream that stole over her more and more often lately. She couldn't beg for a place with her sister if she couldn't find her, and she couldn't find her if she didn't go to that ball.

Gautier had hired Rose. He would know where she was.

Cosette promised herself that the moment he told her, she would walk right out that door and find her, wolves and thieves and soldiers be hanged.

Without second-guessing herself, Cosette hurried over to the quiches, pinched up hers, and scarfed the steaming egg and vegetable tart down in one bite, burning her tongue.

Something told her if she didn't eat it now, she'd come back to find it gone.

4

A MOTHER'S DRESS

osette climbed the back stairs to the servant's quarters, a long line of rooms one after the other at the upmost floor of the Comtesse's château, once bustling with activity, now rendered cold and silent.

She'd been through them multiple times, hunting for anything valuable to use or trade.

Not much was left. But surely something remained that would be useful on trading day.

A few chests. A few moth-eaten garments. Most of the furniture had been used for firewood, once Madame Béatrice had been unable to pay the lad to deliver a cord of wood whenever they were running low.

Cosette scrounged for dead wood—of which there was plenty—but she hated to use it, especially for cooking, due to the stench of the rotting wood.

She stopped as she came into the next room. Her old room.

She'd had her own room downstairs with the rest of the family—at first. Then the last servant had left, and Cosette had burned something.

18

In a rage, Madame Béatrice had demanded she gather her things and take them upstairs.

Cosette had been too frightened to argue.

But now, especially since she rose most days before the rest of the family, she stayed in the little room off the kitchen that had once belonged to the cook, where a measure of warmth could be found.

But she didn't want anyone to know.

Warm one moment, cold the next, sent into a screaming rage at the littlest thing—the Comtesse was so well-liked by her peers, no one would possibly believe how she changed around Cosette . . . except Rose.

Her sister would believe her, would help her escape this awful place. Might even shove her crossbow in Madame Béatrice's face and scare her a little on the way out.

Cosette deflated as reality displaced fantasy.

Non, then the Comtesse would take it out on her girls. Cosette wouldn't do that to them. She would not repay cruelty with revenge.

No matter how often she dreamed of being rescued.

Next, Cosette climbed into the attic, a stuffy room with a single window—a decoration outside that Madame Béatrice did not want displaced, making the servants spend as little time as possible in the broiling room in the summer and freezing room in the winter.

It too had been picked over, but less so than the rest of the house. Almost as if the Comtesse had forgotten the attic existed.

Cosette rifled through trunks, furniture, and cubbies, mentally cataloging what could be used, what could be traded away. What might save them . . . for now.

After moving aside a screen, she gasped aloud. There, under the covering, was a trunk.

But not just any trunk.

Her mère's trunk.

One the Comtesse must have missed.

Cosette's family's things had been the first to go.

With a cry, she fell to her knees, running her fingers along the length of the beloved piece of luggage, surprisingly dust-free after having been buried and forgotten for so long.

Her père must've moved it here when they'd lost their country estate. Despairing, she leaned her head against the trunk and hugged it fiercely. Never mind that her arms wouldn't reach all the way around.

She tugged on the latch, suddenly desperate to see what was inside. It wouldn't budge. Locked.

She bit her lip, blinked back tears, and laid her cheek against the precious wooden and brass container, her heart welling with sudden longing for her mère.

Kind, never raised her voice, elegant—Cosette had only ever wanted to be just like her.

Was she looking down on Cosette from heaven right now? Did she see what Cosette was going through?

Could she not send someone to intercede on Cosette's behalf? It was only what she prayed every day.

So little remained of her memories of her. Her scent, perhaps. The echo of her laugh. Rosette spoke of her as if she remembered every detail. And Cosette...didn't.

It just made Cosette miss her more. Miss both of them more.

When she opened her eyes, her gaze landed on a brass key sticking out of the lock.

Cosette sat upright, feeling a thousand times the fool for not seeing it right away—her family left keys with trunks when stored away, always—and hastened to unlatch it.

With trembling fingers, Cosette opened her mère's trunk.

A waft of herb-scented air rushed over Cosette's face. She pulled out sprigs of lavender and other herbs meant to keep mildew and bugs far away from the cedar chest, and untied a paper-enshrouded garment.

Her mère's dresses!

Cosette dug faster, pulling each garment from its wrappings, letting the rich brocade and satin and tulle fall like luxurious waterfalls of fabric over her lap. Soon she was surrounded by dresses, and memories, from another world, another lifetime.

Hiding at the top of the stairs with Rosette, faces pressed to the banister, soaking in the whirl of bright colors below, the happy chatter, the otherworldly music by the orchestra.

And always the loveliest of all, her mère, the perfect hostess, flitting through the crowds and making sure everyone was comfortable, refreshment in hand, that they knew each other.

Even Rosette's snickering and dry comments about the ridiculous flirting games everyone played weren't enough to pull Cosette from her euphoria. She wanted to *be* down there, dancing, flirting, and wielding her fan to send secret messages to amies and beaux alike.

And deep down she knew Rosette only ridiculed the fêtes because she was deeply insecure about what people thought of her—and her height and gangliness didn't help. Rosette often tripped and broke things. Of course Cosette loved Rose no matter her quirks, and she had grown into her height as a strong, graceful, powerful huntress.

But Cosette would give anything to go back to those days, to be with her mère once more, introduced into a society that welcomed her, not worrying about what to eat next, if they had enough water for the day, if their wood supply would be stolen or run out in the middle of the cold, cold nights.

The last dress came out of the trunk, and Cosette gasped aloud.

Soft, rose-petal pink, airy, light as a dandelion puff—the

dress was perfection. Layer upon layer of sheer light-pink chiffon over shimmering satin . . . Cosette pulled it to her face and breathed deep.

Musty, oui, a little, but it smelled of roses, of her mother's scent, plus the lavender and cedar it had been packed in.

Cosette didn't know how long she sat there, clutching the fabric close, new grief sweeping her with how much she missed her mother. Grief at how the memories were fading, how she couldn't remember her face, her voice.

Just the idea of her.

How the mother she had so hoped for, her new mother, had turned out to be cruel, unlike what a mother should be.

The candle she'd brought with her winked out, plunging Cosette into darkness. It took a moment for her eyes to adjust to the dim light coming from the single window.

Cosette sighed and began to pack up the rich clothes for the town's seamstress, in the hopes she might be willing to trade since Gautier's fête might bring her business. She left the pink vision for last.

The styles had changed so much in the past few years. More crude, far less fabric. Not only did they need hardier stuff to last longer, it was difficult to wash so much fabric, so the long, elaborate dresses with many layers shrank to one or two layers of thicker, scratchy cotton with slimmer, shorter skirts.

Cosette had already begun tucking up her skirts to keep them from dragging on the ground, but she often adjusted their clothing into the newer, slimmer lines with skirts that fell mid-calf.

Her stepsisters had balked at first, but after they had to wash their own clothes a few times, their mère had given Cosette permission to take in and shorten the skirts.

It was so freeing to wear, so much easier to wash.

Even if she did go to the ball, she couldn't justify dirtying her mère's elaborate clothing . . . Cosette froze in the act of putting the pink dress in the bartering pile.

She jumped to her feet, held the dress against herself.

Her mère was taller than Cosette, but not by much. Just enough that the day dress could be taken in in a few places—Cosette was much more petite—and it wouldn't take much to make the dress over into the simpler fashion of today, yet hearkening back to the elegance of before.

She'd make sure it didn't take away from helping the other three women get ready. And it wouldn't cut into their resources, because it belonged to Cosette.

So what if it wasn't a true ballgown? Cosette would make it her own, would think of her mère the whole time she was dancing, feasting—making her way closer to Gautier.

Humming to herself, she spun and twirled around the attic, the rose-pink fabric swirling out from her as she hugged the dress close and danced to an orchestra only she could hear.

5

A DRESS DESTROYED

Cosette spent the next week happily helping the girls redesign their dresses for the ball, taking in their old ballgowns and adding new embellishments as she was able to trade for them.

The town's seamstress was overjoyed to have a reason to do what she loved most, and she was more than happy to trade Cosette's mère's dresses for food for their pantry, as well as exchange little odds and ends for Cosette's lacework.

The lacework seemed to spool from Cosette's fingertips faster than she threaded it, but she didn't mind. There was quite the demand for frilling up old frock coats and ballgowns, and she enjoyed the work.

It was lovely feeling useful again. To work toward a common goal with excitement, not out of fear for survival. For her stepsisters to throw themselves into getting ready, not bickering and fighting and generally making life miserable.

After carefully hiding the food in case anyone tried to steal it from their homestead, Cosette patiently coaxed her stepsisters to sew their own dresses—the work wouldn't get done in time otherwise—while her stepmère refused to let anyone touch her dresses but the seamstress.

The seamstress had to hire more girls to keep up with the work, and the town was abuzz with the good news.

Her stepfamily kept to themselves as much as possible, but Cosette loved the snatches of conversation she had with other villagers as everyone in town got ready in a whirlwind of patched-up clothes and dreams of feasting until they burst.

Then in the evenings, Cosette sat close to the fireplace and worked on her mère's dress. Not much had to be done to it, truly, but there was some patchwork, a few seams had to be taken in, and Cosette took off several inches so it wouldn't drag on the ground.

She was happy.

Then the dresses were done, and the night of the first fête was upon them.

There was a flurry of activity as Cosette helped all three women get ready before Gautier's coach came for them.

Cosette slipped away, cleaned up, pulled her mother's dress over her head, and hurried downstairs. She stopped at the first landing, unable to make herself go any further.

Druce and Stasie nervously fretted in the front parlor, next to the fireplace for warmth but close enough to the front window to see the moment the carriage turned up their drive. They seemed to vibrate as they waited to be swept away to a night of revelry and decadence.

Cosette hated to admit she was scared, but she waited to come down until she heard the carriage turn into their drive.

She glided down the stairs, a beaming smile upon her face. Their fretting quieted, and Druce and Stasie exchanged a glance.

Cosette didn't say anything, just stopped a little ways from them and waited for the coachman to knock on their door.

Both Stasie and Druce looked worried, coming over and staring at the dress.

"Where did you get that?" Stasie asked, then bit her lip.

Druce sneered. "Who cares? What century did it come

from?" She lifted the skirt with two fingers, as if she were afraid to touch it.

Cosette pulled the precious fabric away, hurt blooming in her chest. "It was my mère's. More than adequate to wear to a country ball."

Druce laughed, a disbelieving sound. "You aren't going to the ball."

Cosette lifted her chin, a spark of defiance lighting in her. "I am and I will. All young ladies were invited, no matter their status, and that includes me."

Stasie's brow was still knit in worry. "Are you sure you should? I mean, what if Mère . . . ?" She bit her lip again, as if trying to figure out how to put it. "What if Mère forbids it?"

Cosette turned away, her voice nonchalant, and fretted with her gloves, her heart wringing in worry. "I don't plan on asking her."

"Oh you don't, do you?"

The three girls spun on the woman standing in the doorway, all done up in finery and looking exquisite.

Madame Béatrice slowly looked Cosette up and down. "I see. My, my, my, I do see."

Cosette broke out in a cold sweat. She had so long not been afraid of anything. Even with her père slowly losing himself, leaving his children to fend for themselves, she'd always had her older brothers to look out for her as she'd looked out for her older sisters.

But they were not here now.

Being afraid of someone, someone she lived with, always watching what she said or did, was an entirely new experience for her. Why had her sisters gone off and gotten married? Why had her brothers abandoned her to their new positions?

Why had her père forced her to live with *this* woman?

She would've happily kept house for any of her sisters. The fear, the pain, the betrayal that came with living with her new stepfamily—it was almost unbearable.

Cosette trembled as her stepmère came closer.

Hurry, hurry, she silently urged the carriage oh so slowly making its way to her front door.

Madame Béatrice trailed her finger along Cosette's neckline, circling her like a jackal. "It was fine for its day, I'll give you that, but it needs . . . adjusting."

With a mighty jerk to the back of Cosette's dress, her stepmère tore the overlay of transparent material from her skirt.

Cosette almost fell over but managed to stay upright. She stared in horror at the cloth in her stepmère's hand as she circled back around.

She knew it was old, she'd even repaired a few patches, but it shouldn't have torn that easily, should it have?

"And these split sleeves?" Madame Béatrice fingered them. "So out of fashion."

Rip, rip, and they were gone.

Madame Béatrice continued to circle her, like a wolf trying to distract its prey, degrading the dress, finding fault in each stitch, removing each offending piece.

Cosette didn't do anything, didn't say anything, just stood there and let her mère's exquisite dress be torn from her body.

She couldn't move. She was numb. In shock. No one could truly be that cruel, could they? This wasn't truly happening, was it?

Cosette didn't know how much time had passed, but soon Madame Béatrice stood before her, destroyed dress in her hands, nothing more than a few threads left on Cosette's underclothes.

Stasie and Druce were huddled behind a chair, holding each other, staring at Cosette with wide eyes. They looked horrified, but Cosette couldn't make herself feel anything. She saw the shreds in her stepmère's hands, yet it still wasn't real. It hadn't truly happened.

She was in the midst of a nightmare, nothing more.

She'd wake, she'd cry, and then it would be over.

Please let it be over.

"Oh dear, what shall we do with these rags? We couldn't possibly make something out of them, could we? Much too old. Oh well. They must only be good for burning."

And with those words, Madame Béatrice threw them into the fire with a rage that was palatable.

As if awakening from a trance, Cosette screamed and lunged toward the fireplace, but her stepmère held her back, laughing. Cosette screamed and fought and tried to tear herself free, but she'd never learned to fight, and although she was strong from hard work, her stepmère was stronger.

Once the cloth had blackened and lost its rose-pink color, falling to ash, her stepmère released her, and Cosette fell before the fireplace, plunging her hands into the ashes but pulling them out just as quickly from the heat.

Sobbing, her heart breaking, she raised shaking hands to her face, not caring how much ash she smudged there, not caring that they ached with burns.

"Come, girls," Madame Béatrice said over Cosette's sobs, indifferent. "The carriage is here." She swept from the room, clearly expecting her girls to follow.

Stasie made a broken sound, moving as if to go to Cosette, but Druce pulled her away and whispered furtively. "Non, Stase. She'll punish us next."

Her stepmère's pleasant voice drifted down the hall as she greeted the coachman. "Why, but of course this is all of us. Aren't my girls just lovely this evening? My, but don't you look dapper yourself—"

The girls gently closed the front door.

Cosette stared into the flames.

There was nothing left of her mère's dress. Any of her mère's dresses. Not one stitch. She'd already traded the rest for necessities, and those had surely been altered and sold.

She had nothing but the trunk they had been folded

within, which would most likely be used for firewood when the need became dire. Well, she wouldn't let it. She'd hide it.

The carriage rattled out from in front of the house, down the drive, and through the gate, taking her stepmère and stepsisters to the ball.

Another broken sob burst from her, and Cosette shot to her feet and ran outside. That was it. She wasn't living with her stepmère for one moment longer!

She ran to the edge of their property, then stopped.

Her père's words, "Stay here," and her whispered response, "I promise," drifted on the breeze, and she couldn't make her feet move.

Besides, if she ran away . . . Rose wouldn't be able to find her. She wouldn't be able to talk to Gautier, to find out what had happened to her sister.

Her heart clenched tight in her chest, making it difficult to breathe.

She hadn't heard from Rose in almost a year. Her sister always found a way to leave a note, or to find Cosette and share a snatched and whispered conversation.

But ever since that day in the treehouse, before Père and Cosette had moved, before her sister had accepted that final job from Gautier, Cosette had heard nothing from Ro.

Nothing.

For a *year*.

It wasn't like her.

She didn't know what to do. Whom else to contact. How to find her. And if she left now . . .

She might never see her sister again.

Could she even find her other sisters? Her brothers? The town where they used to live? The journey was long, treacherous. And wolves still hunted, bold in their attacks.

And who knew if her sisters' new husbands would even allow them to take in another mouth to feed?

But to stay and live with . . . that woman? She couldn't

bear it. She simply *had* to speak to this Gautier, no matter what Rose thought of him.

Cosette sank down into the dead weeds and blackened grass that smelled of rot, buried her face in her hands, and cried.

She couldn't leave. She had nowhere to go.

And she wasn't sure she was even brave enough to try.

That was surely why she couldn't make her feet move beyond the stone fence that marked their property's border.

Gautier's soldiers weren't always kind, and a girl traveling on her own—without the skills of a huntress—wouldn't last long. Plus there were still wolves, even with Gautier's efforts.

Did her stepmère know she was being that cruel? Did she not see what she was doing, how she was acting, as wrong? Did she *enjoy* hurting others? What had hurt her so she would act in such a way and then *laugh*?

Cosette didn't understand. She couldn't make herself understand, no matter how hard she tried. Did the Comtesse not want to change? To be better?

"Oh please, please," Cosette whispered through her fingers. "Help me find my sister. Help me leave this awful place. Set these people free from whatever bondage holds them."

Still clad in only her underclothes, too thin for such a cool night, Cosette crawled over to the crumbling stone wall and leaned back against the cold stone.

Glowbugs were out tonight in abundance, something Cosette hadn't seen in an age. They kept flitting around her and into the trees. She leaned her head back and watched them.

How could she go back in there? How could she face them again? She'd never been so humiliated in her life. Never been treated that way before.

"Oh please, Rosette, come home. Come find me."

She closed her eyes.

After what felt like an eternity of sitting there, her heart bleeding, Cosette felt something brush her arm. Her eyes flew open. Glowbugs surrounded her, ruining her night vision, circling her in loops and whirls and jagged lines of light.

She gasped, and they all darted away, as if skittish, then came back, slowly.

She held very still as they circled her, in awe of the little creatures all seeking her out. But . . . they didn't look like normal glowbugs. She couldn't see past their brilliance, but they didn't seem to be shaped like insects.

But try as she might, she never once saw clearly whatever these creatures might be.

She leaned back again and smiled, watching them for as long as they danced for her. Then, suddenly, they all darted away, into the trees.

Cosette sat up, wiped her face, and lifted her chin. She was going to the ball, and no one was going to stop her. Finding Rosette depended upon it.

She climbed to her feet. Taking a shuddering breath, she realized . . . the ache in her heart was gone.

Although she had no solution for what to do about her stepmère and stepsisters, although she still mourned her mère's dress, she wasn't grieving as she had been.

She was simply so very tired. Too tired to feel anything. To make any decisions.

Instead of trying to figure out another way to the ball, instead of going back to the mending or baking or cleaning, Cosette went to the kitchen, stoked the fire, and curled up in her little bed on the other side of the warm bricks.

She fell asleep immediately.

And did not see glowbugs slip in through her window—through cracks sealed against the endless cold weather, cracks that should not have admitted them—to hover gently around her face and comfort her while she slept.

6

A MOST PRECIOUS GIFT

Cosette opened her eyes, instantly alert.

The house was quiet. No one had woken her, demanding breakfast or anything else.

With a start, she realized her hands had stopped aching sometime in the night. Nor were they still deep red with angry burns.

She opened and closed them a few times, thankful they were pain free, wondering how it had happened so quickly.

Then she stretched, got up, and went to investigate.

Carefully opening the first door, she peeked into her step-sisters' room. There, strewn all over the floor, were their simple ballgowns from the night before. Both girls sprawled on their beds, buried deep in covers, and slept the deep sleep of those who had spent the night dancing.

Cosette didn't bother checking on her stepmère. She still hadn't decided what she would do or say the next time she saw the Comtesse.

Hurrying downstairs, Cosette baked bread, fed what animals they had left, and completed the daily tasks that kept her hands busy, if not her mind.

And still last night bothered her. It didn't matter how hard she worked, how much she tried to shove it from her mind, it wouldn't leave her alone.

What her stepmère had done was *wrong*.

But what could Cosette do about it?

Angry at herself for not being able to think of something, angry at the whole situation, Cosette finally grabbed a bucket, her scrub brush, and a cake of soap and took it into the hall.

It didn't really need a scrubbing this soon, but Cosette needed to scrub it.

Thank goodness her hands had stopped hurting.

It was several hours after midday when she heard movement upstairs. She moved on to another section of flooring.

Although she tracked the movements of everyone in the house, as one would if expecting a kick at any moment, she forced herself to ignore them.

Let them get their own breakfast.

The girls came out of their room, saw her, and went down the back stairway to the kitchen. Cosette imagined they ate the hard cheese and twice-baked bread she'd stored in the larder, but she kept telling herself she didn't care.

She was done being their keeper.

Next they went back upstairs, taking a tray if the rattle of dishes and cutlery was anything to go by, only spending mere seconds in their mother's room.

Then they shut themselves up in their own room and were quiet. Very unlike them.

And Cosette scrubbed another section of floor.

Her stepmère never came out of her room, which was just fine by Cosette.

Hours later, Cosette was just about finished, exhausted from scrubbing so hard, when her stepsisters stirred once more. Timidly, quietly, they crept down the main staircase, standing on a section of floor that was dry and clean enough to use as a mirror.

Cosette ignored them.

Finally, Stasie ventured, "The ball lasts for a week."

Cosette knew that.

"We're going again tonight," Druce said in a quiet voice.

"And it's a masked ball."

So help her, if they wanted help with their gowns . . .

"What do I care?" Cosette scrubbed the floor harder. She wasn't about to tell them that's all she'd been thinking about, a way to escape and go anyway. The floor simply hadn't revealed any secrets or plans to her.

"You see, the thing is, well . . . we feel terrible about what happened last night—don't we, Druce? Well, we do. We feel terrible, and we made this for you to make up for it."

Stasie and Druce held out a dress from behind their backs at the same time.

Cosette froze, hardly daring to lift her eyes, to believe that what they were saying was real. That they wouldn't use this moment to further wound her and laugh at her expense.

She lifted her eyes slowly, oh so slowly, afraid of what she might find.

Cosette's mouth fell open. It was tragic, it really was. A hodgepodge of dresses sewn together, colors clashing dismally in a flouncing, flowery, daisy petal–shaped gown, coming just above the ankles. Large stitches pieced the fabrics together, and anyone could see it was made in haste.

Cosette searched their eyes, but both girls were smiling, proud of themselves, hopeful yet unsure. They were not intending to be cruel with this . . . monstrosity.

Cosette studied the dress. Every person at the ball would know it was homemade. That it was done without skill.

But it was the thought. Her stepsisters had done something kind. For *her*.

Tears filled Stasie's eyes, and even Druce swallowed and looked down. "She should never have torn nor burned your mère's dress, Cosette. We are truly so very sorry."

Cosette dropped her scrub brush into the bucket, climbed

to her feet, and walked over to her sisters. She fingered the gown, recognizing many of their dresses she'd had to wash in her time here. Most of the fabric was from the hems they'd cut off to make the dresses last longer, but Cosette didn't care.

She threw her arms around both girls. "Oh, *merci*. I can't tell you how much this means to me."

Stasie was quick to hug her back, but Druce's arms came up much more slowly.

"Can you ever forgive us?" Stasie asked, her voice thick with tears.

Cosette pulled back. "Forgive you? For what?"

Not that they didn't have anything to ask forgiveness for —Cosette just wondered for *which* thing they were asking.

"For not doing anything, not saying anything—not trying to stop it," Stasie said, her eyes begging for pardon.

"Oui," Druce said quietly. "And for being cruel ourselves."

She put her hands behind her back and wouldn't look up from the floor.

"Of course I forgive you!" Cosette cried, flinging her arms around them once more and squeezing tight. "This is all I have ever wanted, from the first moment I met you—for us to be sisters."

Stasie gave in to her tears, and even a few from Druce dripped on Cosette's shoulder, but Cosette's smile couldn't be stopped. She looked up at the ceiling and mouthed "Merci" to the heavens.

Her prayers couldn't have been better answered.

Druce pulled back, worried. "You won't tell her, will you? What we did."

Druce instantly looked ashamed of herself, but she didn't take back the question, and she eyed the dress as if debating whether to snatch it back.

Cosette couldn't blame her. Either of them, really, for Stase looked just as worried.

She shook her head. "Non, I promise."

Once again, her words held weight, just as freshly shocking now as it was each time such a thing happened.

She needed to *think* before she said such things.

Not that she regretted this particular promise—but she also didn't want to trap herself into saying something she couldn't take back, either.

Druce looked relieved, as did Stasie.

"How will you get to the ball tonight?" Stasie asked.

"Oh, don't you worry none, ma chère." Cosette winked. "I have my ways. Now, off with you both. Shoo! Wash your faces and get ready." She smiled lovingly at them both. "I have my own preparations to make."

"We're not the only ones who need to wash up." Druce smirked. "You'll be mistaken for a cinder girl."

At Cosette's blank look, Druce gestured to her cheeks and forehead. "There's quite a lot of ash on your face still. From last night."

The three girls sobered at that, each lost in their own thoughts.

"Make food," Stasie said suddenly. "Before we go, I mean. If you do everything normally, well, perhaps she won't think anything's amiss?"

Cosette nodded her agreement, and the girls hurried upstairs.

She started for the kitchen and her little room to the side of it, where she often slept because the bricks next to the little cot stayed warm from the backside of the fireplace.

Cosette closed the door behind her and started to lay the dress on the bed.

But the garish monstrosity in her hands stopped her.

There was no way she'd get close to Gautier in this. Dieu, she didn't even want to be *seen* in this.

It just needed a little fixing. Here, there, and right here. The jagged cuts of the pieced-together cloths smoothed. Thick threads were made dainty and slick, undulating through the cloth as if they glided through, practically invisible instead of knotted and so obviously . . . there.

The daisy petal–shaped ruffles on the skirt needed to be rounded into more . . . tulip shapes, perhaps? And these colors would never do.

What if they were softened into a rainbow of pastels, each strip bleeding into the other as if it had been done on purpose?

And the scratchiness of the homespun next to the decadence of tulle and silk — perhaps something in the middle. Chiffon? Light, breezy, airy — she'd need a satin underlay.

Just like her mère's dress.

She held the new dress to her chest, her mourning swift and sudden, and let herself feel her loss until the sensation lessened.

Then she peeked inside, smoothed the course cotton there into satin, and went back to fixing the petals into chiffon.

She stood back. It was unlike anything she'd ever seen. Almost as if . . . fairies . . . had made it.

Cosette laughed and shook the thought away, then hid the dress so her stepmère couldn't find it.

All she had to do was wait for her stepfamily to leave for the ball, then she'd hurry and change. She could even use the old Domino masque she'd found in the attic. Maybe add some lace to it so she'd be harder to recognize.

Then she'd sneak into the ball, and she'd speak to Gautier. She wouldn't leave till she had.

Her jaw tightened. She'd deal with her stepmère later. Then her shoulders slumped.

She just didn't know how.

7

ESCAPE TO A BALL

Cosette gave her stepfamily time to forget something and come back—which they hadn't and didn't—and then what she hoped was plenty of time to reach the ball before getting ready herself.

As she entered her little room, something glowed on the bed. She put up her arm to block the powerful light.

The same lights that had surrounded her in the garden, that had comforted her after her stepmère had torn her dress to shreds, darted off the bed and out the window. The closed window.

But Cosette couldn't take her eyes off the bed.

On it rested the most beautiful pair of shoes she'd ever seen.

Slowly, she picked up one and breathed out, "Oh!"

The dancing slipper appeared to be made of glass, but in the same pastel pattern as her dress. Its small heel was perfect for spinning around a dance floor all night.

She turned it every which way in the moonlight, and it shimmered a rainbow of colors.

"Oh!" she said again, unable to articulate how lovely they were, or her surprise at finding them there.

She hurried over and opened the window. "Merci beaucoup!" she called to whoever had left them.

Lights that she thought were reflected moonlight on the bush next to her window disengaged and fled into the trees.

She smiled and closed the window, cradling the shoe to her chest. It would match her dress perfectly.

She quickly washed up and fixed her hair in an exquisite updo, her fingers flying through intricate braids and weaving strands into submission with hardly any effort.

Rose had always been pouty about Cosette's ability to make masterpieces out of hair strands, but that's just how it was. Cosette only had to picture what she wanted to do with someone's hair, and her fingers simply knew to do it. Cosette smiled at the memory of fixing her sisters' hair before their fêtes.

Then she reverently took her stepsisters' gift and draped it over her head. It fit perfectly.

It had previously tied in the back, but Cosette had fixed that too, with small laces on either side of the bodice. She pulled them to fit her figure and then tied them off so that the laces were hidden under the skirt's petals.

It never even crossed her mind to find it odd that she could change little things like this. That's just how it always had been. Certain things came easy for her, but it was always silly nonsense like clothes or shoes.

Speaking of shoes . . .

She held her breath and turned—the shoes were still on the bed.

She settled onto the creaky frame and thin mattress, picking up both shoes and once more lifting her eyes to the heavens. "Merci," she whispered. And slipped them on.

The glass was sticky? Non, more like squishy? On the inside. It cradled her feet and formed itself to her shape. Cosette quickly tied the ribbons around her ankles and stood, taking a few practice steps.

Whatever was on the inside gave with each step, cushioning her foot, more comfortable than any other shoe she'd owned in her life.

Oh, if only other shoes could be like this! she thought.

She danced the minuet around her small room a few times, but the glass never bit into either foot. Whatever cushioned them was simply delightful, and Cosette was entranced.

Now to get to the ball in plenty of time to talk to Gautier.

She ran right out the door, down the road, and past the boundary line, her skirts trailing behind her like streamers, her heart lightening with every step.

8

RECOGNIZED

*A*lthough she searched for every opportunity, she couldn't get anywhere near Gautier. The crush had him surrounded, adored, vying for his attention at every turn.

Cosette wasn't even certain what he looked like, she was kept so far away.

She certainly hoped it wasn't like this every night, but she comforted herself that she had five more nights to try.

She *would* get what she came for. Even if it wasn't on this very night.

It somewhat soothed her pride that she danced the night away. She didn't draw too much attention—she was one of hundreds come for feasting and forgetfulness from such hard lives—but she never wanted for a partner, and she absolutely gorged herself on food she didn't have to slave over to prepare.

She kept a wary eye out for her stepmère, hopeful her masque and dress were enough of a disguise, but not putting it past the woman to recognize her no matter what she wore.

Then, suddenly, the worst happened.

One of her partners stole her masque, laughing and calling behind him that he would remember her always, but no

41

matter how desperately she tried to get it back, she couldn't find whoever had stolen it in the crowd.

She had to get away before her stepmère saw her.

As she was leaving, Gautier got up on a balustrade—it was already the wee hours of the morning—and announced all the food would be going home with the guests, as it would every night of the ball, to much cheering and a general stampede out the door to collect their treasure and hoard it away at home.

That was one way to clear a room.

Cosette laughed, completely forgetting her fear in the joy of the moment, and clapped and cheered with the rest of the guests, letting herself be carried away with the crowd and out the door to gather her own pillage.

A perfect end to a lovely evening.

Cosette couldn't wait to come back.

As the austere butler stuffed her arms full of food already prepared for departing guests—most likely so the guests wouldn't also carry off the family silver—Cosette laughed again, she couldn't help it, and said, "Merci beaucoup, Monsieur! May Dieu bless your very soul for such kindness."

He gave her a stiff nod and was already turning to the next guest when Cosette's gaze caught and held on a woman staring at her. With a cold, hard glare. Absolute fury in her eyes.

Madame Béatrice.

With Druce and Stase standing behind her, arms stuffed full, faces pale and expressions horrified.

Cosette went cold all over.

Then she was jostled aside by others wanting their share, and her stepfamily was lost to the crowd.

Cosette turned and ran all the way home, terrified that her stepfamily would find her on the road and run her down with the carriage.

Hopefully the crush kept them away for hours yet.

9

FOUND OUT

In a frenzy, Cosette hid all the food, hoping she remembered where she'd put it and didn't accidentally let any of it go to waste, then hurried out of her clothes and shoes and hid them in the servant's quarters.

This is where she was, what she was doing, when the carriage rumbled up to the Comtesse's château.

Cosette tried to run, tried to hide, but the Comtesse found her first.

Flying at her, Madame Béatrice grabbed a fistful of Cosette's hair and slammed her against the wall. "You would dare defy me? In my own home? In my own community? After I have fed you and sheltered you and clothed you. This is how you repay me?"

Cosette gasped, unable to think of anything to say, fear shutting her mind fast.

Madame Béatrice suddenly released her, and Cosette fell to the ground and raised her hands to shield herself.

"Drucelle, get me the cane."

Druce balked, looking to her sister for support. "Maman, please . . ."

Madame Béatrice spun on her daughter, teeth bared in a

43

snarl. "I didn't ask you to beg for my pardon! Get the cane, Drucelle. Or I shall use it on you first."

Druce and Stasie fled together.

Madame Béatrice turned back to Cosette and crossed her arms. "Where's the dress?"

Cosette just gasped and shook her head, eyes wide, heart pounding, unable to form words or make herself get up.

"I swear to you I will tear apart every room in this house—"

The thought of all that work filled Cosette's mind, something for her to cling to in the storm. "It wasn't . . . the dress . . . it wasn't mine . . ."

As in, it was made of her stepsisters' dresses, and hadn't been hers previously, before they'd given it to her, but of course Cosette couldn't tell her that.

Although Cosette could not tell an outright lie—had never been able to, in fact—twisting the truth . . . that was another matter entirely.

A single eyebrow climbed the Comtesse's face. "So you stole it, then, did you? I'm not even a little surprised."

"Non, I swear to Dieu, I would never!"

She got right in Cosette's face, and Cosette slammed her eyes shut. "Where's the dress, Cosette? I won't stop asking till you tell me, I won't stop looking till it's in my hands."

Cosette shook her head, keeping her eyes tightly closed, somehow knowing that if her stepmère found the dress, she'd see the many dresses her daughters had sewn into it, that the magic of the dress would have faded by now, that Druce and Stasie would be cowering next.

She couldn't let that happen.

"Very well."

The absolute coldness, the emptiness of all humanity, chilled Cosette to her very bones.

"If you continue to defy me, you will be locked in your room for the remainder of the fête. If you cannot honor and obey me, your own mother, by law if not by choice, then I can't trust you, can I?"

Cosette's eyes flew open, and she stared at her stepmère, horrified. *You are not my mother!*

She just barely kept the words from bursting past her lips and said instead, "But, but — Gautier invited everyone to the ball! Even servants and, and peasants!"

A malicious smile curled Madame Béatrice's lips. "We certainly know which category you fall into, don't we? But the fact remains: If I can't trust you to do as I say, then I shall have to ensure you can do no other."

She yelled down the hallway, "Where is that cane?"

At no answer from her girls, she turned back with a huff. "I suppose I'll have to go after it myself, shan't I?"

She hauled Cosette to her feet, pushed her into the broom closet, and shoved something under the door.

Cosette could only stare at the door in horror, and after her stepmère's footsteps faded away, stare about the dark space in disbelief.

Aside from a broom, a bucket, and a few cleaning rags, the small space was deserted, and so very cold. Cosette would freeze in here, even if the sun was just now peeking over the horizon.

How long would her stepmère keep her locked away?

Backing up until she hit the wall, she slid down it and buried her face in her skirts, whispering, "My sister is coming. She *will* come for me. Then I'll wake to find this only a dream. A horrible, terrible, nightmarish dream."

But it was getting harder and harder to believe the stories she told herself.

10

GEMS, PETALS, AND PEARLS

ack and legs aching, Cosette hobbled past her stepsisters on the way out of the house. They were quiet, sullen, eyes rimmed in red.

"You couldn't leave well enough alone, could you?" Druce muttered at her back.

Cosette gasped and spun toward her. "What did you say?"

Stasie looked between them quickly, but she settled on Druce's side. "You couldn't have better hid? Or at least kept your masque on?"

Cosette threw out her hands, winced, and drew them stiffly back to her sides. "You don't think I tried? Someone stole it from me as a keepsake." She winced again, this time at the memory. "I promise you I tried to get it back."

The girls stared at her, eyes hollow.

"And I was watching, she just—she saw me first." Cosette deflated. "If I had only left sooner, not stopped for any food . . ."

The girls didn't say another word, their silence stony and their glares weighing on Cosette like a physical burden. So she turned and left.

She would have to make it up to them. Somehow.

46

Cosette limped toward the well in the forest, eyes gritty from too many tears and too little sleep.

It wasn't the first time she'd had a cane taken to her legs, but the hurt in her chest was almost more than she could bear.

No matter what she did, no matter how hard she worked, no matter what strides she made to befriend her stepsisters, her stepmère swiped it away with a few cruel words. Or a beating.

Her stepsisters were just as terrified of their mother as she was, Cosette could see it in their eyes, but they always chose their mother's side, and they had learned kindness never turned out well for them.

If only Cosette could make them see there was a better way!

If only Rose would come back and help her. Rescue her from this horrid house.

Cosette choked on a sob, leaned against the closest tree, and gave in to her tears.

Why did Rosette have to leave? Her sister was her best friend, and if only their père hadn't thrown her out for being a huntress—non. She couldn't go there.

The heartache, the sadness would pull her under, for who knew how long this time, and she must remain hopeful. She must believe there were better things to come.

Dabbing her tears on her apron, she trudged on toward the well. The welts on her legs ached with every step, and her chest felt hollowed out, empty.

As she walked, a few birds trailed her, winging around her in loops, and several field mice and squirrels bounded alongside her.

As they usually did.

But she'd forgotten to grab a handful of crumbs, and she didn't have the heart to speak to them in her broken voice. She'd just start crying again.

They'd simply have to be satisfied with her presence this time.

Halfway there, she stepped into the woods, removed her stockings, and shoved them deep into her pockets. She couldn't stand them rubbing against her wounds, especially the ones that oozed. She'd have to soak them off if her stockings dried to them, and she simply didn't have time for that.

Still sniffling a little, trying to ignore the pain in her heart, Cosette reached the well, moved the twisting vines she'd coaxed into place to hide it, and drew crisp, clear water, carefully filling her buckets so she wouldn't spill a drop.

Thank goodness she'd discovered this well when she had.

It was most definitely a pain to draw water from—the well was deep and the bucket heavy; her arms ached by the time she'd drawn two buckets—but their household wouldn't have survived without it.

Cosette stopped, dropped her head, and leaned against the well with her arms braced on the low, cold stone.

She simply *had* to get close enough to Gautier to speak with him. What began as a half-formed plan became an obsession.

No one had heard of Rosette's whereabouts in an age. Except Gautier. And Cosette had no way to ask him before— but now he was in her world. The guest of honor at the highest local nobleman's estate. All she had to do was capture a dance with him, smile prettily, and ask him.

She *had* to go back to that ball! Her future depended upon it.

The last thing Rose had said to her was that she was hunting for Gautier. All of her sister's reservations aside, he was doing his best to put this country back together and stop the curse. Rose had hunted for him for two years, rising swiftly in the ranks to trusted huntsman, and then silence. Not a word.

She'd simply disappeared.

Cosette must meet Gautier. She must. If only to find out what he knew.

"May I have a drink, my dear?"

Cosette startled and dropped the bucket. It clanged all the way down and splashed into the water below, and she quickly peered over to see if she'd broken it. But of course it was too dark to tell.

She turned toward the voice to find a wizened old woman sitting on a log near the well, leaning heavily on her walking staff.

"Pardon?" she asked, slightly flustered.

"May a tired old woman have a refreshing drink?"

Cosette's manners came back in droves. She dipped a slight curtsey. "Why, most definitely, old mother. Have you a skin?"

The old woman held up a waterskin from over her shoulder.

Cosette offered her sweetest smile. "I will draw that for you now." And she'd check on the bucket at the same time.

Her arms froze several times, shaking, before she hauled a full bucket over the rim. A gust of relief left her when she saw the bucket was no worse for her mishandling of it, and she carefully filled the woman's waterskin without spilling a drop.

"May I do anything else for you while I'm here, old mother?"

The old woman tipped back the skin and drank deeply, nearly emptying it. She sighed and swiped water from her lips, then held up the waterskin again.

"Top it off?"

Cosette smiled, though it was a bit strained—she was concerned her arms would give out and she'd splash water all over the old woman, and it was too cold to leave her soaking wet—and now her legs were starting to shake from the pain. And the exhaustion. And her hunger.

She filled the skin again, then stepped back and waited while the woman once again guzzled like a camel.

"Will that be all?" she asked kindly, once the woman had finished and could talk.

The old woman eyed her, and as soon as even Cosette thought about squirming, she flicked her fingers and turned her back on Cosette. "That will be all. Off with you."

Cosette went still for half a heartbeat as numerous thoughts assaulted her at once. Could no one in this entire curse-ridden kingdom be kind? How much more could she endure?

But it wasn't up to her how others treated her. It was up to *her* how she treated *them*.

And if her mother could be kind under all circumstances, well then, so could she.

She took a deep breath, let it out slowly, and dipped her final curtsey. "Then I wish you the best of days, Madame."

Cosette tied the bucket in place, secured the well covering —so that no one could fall in and be hurt, and so that nothing could contaminate the water—and hid the well once more. And if the old woman gossiped about their well and told others where to find it? Cosette sighed. A worry for another day. She was simply too weary.

Then she settled the heavy water buckets across her shoulders.

Her wounds twinged, threatened to split open again. She'd have to move carefully.

Also, she couldn't spill a drop—it would take every measure of her dancing lessons to make the journey home as smooth as possible. If only her legs didn't throb so.

She was partway down the road when the old woman called after her, "Young Mademoiselle, do you want nothing in return?"

Cosette came to a gradual stop and shuffled partway

around to be able to speak without shouting and while making eye contact. "I wish for you to have a pleasant day."

She smiled to show she meant the strained words, that it was her burden and not the old woman that was wearing on her, and tried to turn back to her task.

"Are you certain? Nothing at all?"

Cosette started to pant as she held still. As long as she was moving, she could take the next step. Tell herself all she had was just one more step. But standing here, straining under the weight—she wouldn't be able to hold out much longer.

She blinked rapidly. "Only to be on my way, and if you ever have need of me again, you need only ask."

"Wait."

With the third interruption, it was all Cosette could do not to burst into tears. Tears that would turn into great, heaving sobs. She was so tired. And everything hurt. And she missed her sister.

"Perhaps we should start with your legs?"

Cosette blinked at the old woman, much like Rose did when startled, but she couldn't make the words make sense. "What about my legs?"

She met the woman's eyes, and suddenly, her legs no longer hurt. There was no great change, no whirlwind and no angel coming down in glory, but her legs simply stopped aching.

Cosette cried out and carefully, oh so carefully, set down her buckets. And lifted her skirts.

Her legs were a smooth, healthy pink, with no bruises, cuts, or welts in sight.

"Oh, merci! Merci beaucoup!"

Cosette ran to the woman and threw her arms around her.

The old woman laughed and patted Cosette's back, a little awkwardly. She said, "And why don't we take care of those water buckets, just for today?"

Cosette pulled back and turned wide eyes to the road. Her buckets were simply gone. "Where are they?"

"Why, in your kitchen, but of course."

She'd heard stories of such things happening—she'd thought they were fiction, of course—but she was so excited to see it with her own eyes, she didn't even question the magic.

Of course, it was entirely possible she was still standing at the lip of the well, staring into the woods, lost in her daydreams.

But it certainly felt real.

Cosette shook her head, her smile nearly splitting her face. "There aren't words in our beautiful language to thank you enough. Shall you come home with me? I would so love to make you a meal, let you place your feet up by my hearth, to see you on your way rested and full."

It would hardly begin to repay her for her kindness, but it was all Cosette had to offer.

The woman cupped Cosette's cheek in her hand. "You are a dear, dear child."

Cosette smiled back, happier than she'd been in a long time.

Kindness was how love made itself known to her. The little things, the small things, they all added up into something glorious, and Cosette lived to experience it. And this woman had done so much more besides.

Moisture entered the old woman's eyes, but she blinked it away and pulled back.

Cosette was instantly stricken. "Oh, did I hurt you, grand-mère? Perhaps when I hugged you?"

The old woman waved Cosette's words away and chuckled thickly. "Call me a senile old fool, but your happiness has touched this old woman's heart. Might I give you a boon?"

A boon? Was this woman the answer to all her hopes and dreams coming true?

Cosette's heart leaped into her eyes, and she clasped her hands under her chin. "Oh, might you? I have lost someone dear to me, my sister, the huntress Rosette LeFèvre. She means everything to me, and what I want most in this world is to see her again. Can you tell me where she is? How to find her, perhaps? Or who can help me find her?"

But the old woman was already shaking her head. "I cannot, I'm afraid, but I can do better."

Now Cosette's eyes filled with tears. All she wanted was to see her sister again. To know if she lived or had . . . passed on. Cosette felt sick at the thought.

She could think of nothing better than seeing Rosette's dear face.

"Tell you what. If you need me, come find me. Right here, in these woods. And make your request."

Cosette nodded, her entire heart breaking. Could no one help her find the huntress?

"Until then"—the woman smiled, the most beautiful smile Cosette had ever seen, entirely shocking on a woman of her age, then leaned close and whispered in her ear—"for your kindness to me, for your sweet spirit and kind nature, every word you speak will reflect your heart."

She pulled back and cupped Cosette's face in her gnarled hands.

"When you speak, flowers and pearls and every precious gem this world has to offer will drip from your tongue, to build your wealth for when you need it most."

She laid a hand over Cosette's heart.

"And your burden will be lifted for a little while. Nothing but joy shall permeate you, to keep you warm in spite of all the dreariness that surrounds you."

Cosette's eyes widened, and she meant to object, she really did, but the next thing she knew, her eyes were opening, a bird sang outside her window, and weak sunlight shone through the glass onto her bedspread.

She smiled and stretched. What a lovely dream. If only it had been real.

Cosette could use such kindness in her life.

At least it came to her in dreams, if nowhere else.

Heart light, a smile on her lips, she climbed out of bed, got ready for her day, made her breakfast, fed what barn animals they had left, and awaited her stepmère calling for her own breakfast. She hummed to herself as she worked.

Her stepsisters were nowhere to be found.

Well past noon, the servant bells began ringing, and Cosette carried the Comtesse's tray up first. "Good morning, stepmère," Cosette said with a beaming smile, and a diamond, two pearls, and a rose petal fell onto her stepmère's breakfast tray.

She froze. Her stepmère froze. They eyed each other. Then the tray.

"What," her stepmère asked, "has just happened?"

"I couldn't possibly begin to guess," she said honestly.

A shower of rubies, sapphires, and emeralds joined their siblings upon the tray.

Faster than Cosette had ever seen her move, her stepmère was out of her bed and upon her, Cosette's ear firmly in her grasp. She wrenched painfully, and Cosette cried out and dropped her tray to a tremendous crash of dishes.

A pause, then running footsteps. Her stepmère shouted "Out!" the minute the door was pushed open, and Cosette's stepsisters retreated.

But she could hear them just on the other side of the door.

Madame Béatrice led Cosette by her ear and shoved her into the nearest chair. "Sit! And stay."

Then the cruel woman bent over the fallen tray and carefully removed each gem from among the shards of porcelain, leaving the rose petals where they lay.

After inspecting each jewel with a little cry or crooning or some other noise of pleasure, Madame Béatrice shoved the handful under Cosette's nose. "Explain right now, or so help me, I will cane you for stealing."

Cosette's mouth popped open, but it was several seconds before she could speak. "I would *never*—"

More precious jewels, flower petals, and pearls slid from her lips to pool in her lap.

The Comtesse cried out and dropped most of what she held to gather what had fallen. She hurried to a jewelry box, shoved both fistfuls in, then was on her hands and knees, gathering every glittering stone and pearl that had rolled onto the floor.

Cosette could only watch with wide eyes.

What was happening? Did that mean the dream was real? That she'd actually met an old woman in the woods?

Then why did it feel so distant? So hazy. As if she walked in a cloud, and everything around her hardly existed.

She couldn't even fathom where the jewels were coming from. She felt nothing in her mouth—nothing—but with every word she spoke, loveliness dripped from her tongue in elegant waves.

Reflecting her words. Reflecting her heart.

There was only one explanation: the woman was a fairy. Or a witch. But Cosette felt fairy was much more apt. She hoped.

All this flashed in her mind in the time it took her step-mère to show her greed.

Now she was back, and before Cosette could lift a finger to protect herself—not that she would—she always froze in stressful situations, while it was Rosette's first instinct to protect or attack—her stepmère grabbed a handful of her blonde curls, hauled her to her feet, and held their faces close.

"Tell me everything. Now."

11

NEW WEALTH, NEW DRESSES

lifetime of tears later, Cosette sat next to the fireplace, ashes staining her skirt, and sobbed.

As her stepsisters watched.

Jewels didn't fall from her lips as she cried or made noises —only when she spoke. And her stepmère had quite the collection of gems now that she'd forced Cosette to tell her everything.

No matter how close she got to the warmth, to the flames, she still shivered and shook, ice filling her core.

Even as her stepmère had rained cruelty upon her head, Cosette was filled with hope that she'd see what she was doing, that she was overreacting, that Cosette was innocent.

The feeling of lightness, of hope that things would get better and this was all just a misunderstanding, persisted until her stepmère struck her, right near the end, trying to get the exact location of the well.

Not that Cosette had ever hidden it from her family. They were simply too lazy to get the water they needed for them-selves. And she couldn't explain *where* the well was—just that her feet found it in the woods every time she needed it.

An answer her stepmère in no way appreciated.

Something in her had broken then, her memories of the horrors of the last few days flooding back in, and Cosette had burst into tears and been unable to stop.

It seemed such a cruel trick of the fairy to make her forget —the remembering was then so much worse.

The Comtesse had hauled her downstairs in disgust, thrown her next to the fireplace, and commanded her daughters to watch Cosette like twin raptors.

Under strict orders to capture anything that fell from her lips, her stepsisters stood just inside the kitchen, close to the door in case they needed to escape, and watched Cosette sob her heartache out.

She'd never missed her mother—and her sister—more, and she'd do anything to have them both back. She'd never ask for anything else if she could just have that one thing.

"Cosette . . ." Stasie started even as Druce shushed her.

"We're not supposed to talk to her, remember?"

Stasie clamped her lips shut.

Cosette cried until she couldn't wring another drop of moisture from her eyes, then sat there and hiccuped, staring into the flame she was supposed to be cooking their supper over. But she couldn't make herself care, and she couldn't make herself begin to cook.

A rustle of skirts proceeded Madame Béatrice. "Girls, put on your finest clothes." To Cosette she said, "Upstairs, now. And I want the key to your room."

Cosette couldn't make herself look up from the fire.

"Where are we going, Maman?" Stasie asked hesitantly, softly.

"Who cares?" Druce put in defiantly, her attitude instantly changing at the appearance of her mother. "We have another chance to dress up! I'm not letting that pass me by."

Drucelle tried to haul Stasie out of the room, but Stasie remained where she was, her eyes on the Comtesse. "And what are going to do with Cosette?" she asked, even more softly.

"None of your business," Madame Béatrice snapped. "Now go. Before I lose my temper."

Druce tugged on Stasie until she relented, but Cosette could feel the sisters' eyes on her as they left.

Well, fled, more like.

"Come with me," Madame Béatrice demanded.

"Listen to your stepmère" echoed in her père's voice, followed by her foolish, foolish "I promise."

Wordlessly, Cosette got up and followed without really meaning to, too wrung out to particularly care what happened to her.

They traversed to the third floor, where the servants used to live—where Cosette had claimed a room before she'd started sleeping in the cook's quarters off the kitchen. Where it was warmer.

Madame Béatrice opened the door and held out her hand. "Key."

Cosette took the keyring from the chatelaine at her waist and started to remove the key to her old room.

Her stepmère made a surprised noise, as if she hadn't considered that Cosette was now the housekeeper, scullery maid, gardener, and every other position they'd had to let go over the time they'd all lived together.

It had been more bearable when her stepsisters had truly made an effort to help. When her stepmère hadn't undone Cosette's every effort.

"All of them, if you please."

Cosette placed the keys into her stepmère's outstretched hand and slipped into her room, one she hadn't slept in in an age, not that she'd tell her stepmère that.

The Comtesse wouldn't meet her eyes as she fumbled through the keyring, searching for the right key.

"Where are you taking them?" Cosette asked, concerned

what latest torment the Comtesse had planned for her daughters.

"The keys?" Madame Béatrice cocked her head, looking briefly bemused, a frown marring the smooth skin of her face.

"Non. Stasie and Drucelle."

Madame Béatrice's eyes gleamed, and she answered, though Cosette hadn't really expected it. "Thanks to your . . . affliction . . . I am taking the girls into town for new dresses, now that we can afford them."

Cosette heart skipped a beat. What if they told someone where they got the jewels? How long until someone else sought to kidnap her and lock her up for their own profit? Chances were the next person to try to own her would be even less kind, if that were possible.

As if she read her thoughts, her stepmère continued with a sneer. "You needn't worry about *that*. As long as you give me your jewels, you will have a place here, and no one else need know of your . . . affliction."

Cosette highly regretted meeting the old woman in the woods, though she couldn't quite make herself regret being kind. She still would've done so, but she in no way would've accepted anything from her.

Nor would she ever again.

"And then"—the gleam in her stepmère's eyes grew tenfold, and Cosette could picture her cackling and rubbing her hands together—"my own girls will go into the woods, dressed as peasants, and receive their own boon from the old woman." Her greed morphed into intense hate, directed at Cosette. "And then we shall have no more need of *you*."

She slammed the door, the bolt sliding home with the rattle of keys, and Cosette stared at the door in shock. In pain.

What had she done to make her stepmère hate her so? To hate them all so?

And what did she mean, "have no more need of you"? She wouldn't . . . dispose . . . of Cosette, would she? Surely not.

Non, not as long as gems fell from her mouth with every word, no matter if her daughters were able to do the same.

Cosette went still.

Stasie. Drucelle. They were never kind.

And if the old woman were a fairy—and honest-to-Dieu fairy—then she would smell out a lie a kilomètre away.

And if she were a witch . . .

The girls wouldn't stand a chance either way. She had to warn them. She started searching for something, anything, to use to pick the lock.

12

NEW SERVANTS

Finding nothing, Cosette spent most of her time staring out the single round decorative window, hurrying them back with every piece of her soul.

The room was freezing, no blankets to be had, and although this was one of the few servant's quarters with a fireplace, there was nothing to burn. No way to strike it if there were.

So she huddled close to the window, begging the heavens for warmth, shivering and wondering how long it could possibly take to commission new dresses. Did they expect to have them in time for tonight's ball?

She didn't know, but she couldn't see how it could be done.

Then again, with Gautier bringing food, perhaps gems were worth something once more.

She was nodding off, eyes closing all on their own, cheek pressed against the window sill, when the old carriage they kept in their barn came rattling back.

She sat up. Pressed her face to the glass. Did they have a horse now? And had the axle been fixed? She always had to walk to the village for what they needed.

Cold fear washed over her. Just how much wealth had her stepmère flashed around their starving and poor neighbors? And how long until someone came looking to deprive them of it?

Cosette strained to follow the carriage's path, but once it came to rest in front of the small château, she could no longer see it. But she could hear new voices. High-pitched. Two of them. New serving girls?

Cosette distinctly heard Madame Béatrice say, "I will show you girls to your rooms, then you can make us tea."

She sat up, hopeful that she would be released soon.

But non. No footsteps came her way, and no one came to her rescue.

Her stepmère's words washed over her once more. "And then we'll have no more need of *you.*"

She curled up, buried her face in her knees, and hoped her stepmère stayed far away.

13

RELEASED

*H*er stepmère didn't come for her that evening. Or all the next day.

Cosette slept as much as she could, shivering and starving, the ache in her belly feeling like it was carving her out.

And she was so *thirsty*. Had they forgotten her?

It was late the next day, when Cosette was weak from hunger and almost sick with thirst, that she heard something.

Footsteps. A scratching at her door.

Cosette bolted to her feet and took a few steps before dizziness swamped her. She lurched to the wall, clinging to it, thinking too late that if it were her stepmère, she shouldn't be so close to the door.

Stasie peeked in, her eyes darting around the sparse room, looking everywhere but at Cosette. Unmitigated relief swept Cosette, and she let out a choked sob.

"Oh, there you are." Stasie looked rather uncomfortable, not quite meeting Cosette's eyes. "Maman says you need to draw the water."

Cosette nodded fiercely, willing to do anything to get out of this room. She swallowed hard, trying to make words form past her dry throat.

"Water . . . do you have . . . ?"

A few gems fell from her mouth, and Cosette fumbled to catch them. She handed them to Stasie before she could ask for them.

Stasie shoved them in her apron's pocket. "All out, désolé." She looked further embarrassed. "And, uh, we don't know where the well is, so . . ."

Cosette took a moment to steady herself, then started down the hall, growing stronger with every step. She just had to get to the well, guzzle water, and then find that old woman and beg her not to harm her stepsisters.

"And then Maman says you should do the mending, in case our dresses aren't done in time for tonight."

Cosette turned back, her thoughts sluggish. "Is there no one else to . . . help?" She could've sworn she heard other voices when they came back yesterday.

Three jewels, a rose petal, and a pearl fell from her lips.

With a sigh, Cosette handed them over.

A blush stole over her stepsister's face as she pocketed the wealth. "There were. New servants, I mean. They, ah, didn't last the day. One of them said they didn't know how the, uh, other servant managed it all. By herself." Stasie ducked her head.

Cosette nodded, wishing she had someplace else to run off to as well.

"Also . . ." Stasie dug around her in apron's pocket and came out with a small pouch on a string. It had a wide mouth. She thrust it toward Cosette. "Mère said to put this on while you're not"—her eyes flicked to the chamber Cosette had just come from—"well, you know."

Clamping her jaw tight against a protest of how unfair it all was, Cosette accepted the pouch and tied it on. The string was just long enough to tuck it into her neckline, its wide mouth gaping just below her chin.

Cosette felt ridiculous. And humiliated.

And determined not to say another word.

"I wouldn't blame you," Stasie said as Cosette started to turn away. "If you . . . hurried out . . . and, well. Just kept going."

Cosette eyed her in surprise.

Stasie shrugged, looking years older with the weariness that crept into her eyes. "In case you were thinking of such a thing."

Fear swept over Cosette, that if Stasie knew her secret thoughts, that if Stasie could see her longing . . .

If Stasie suspected, did her stepmère?

She spun and made her way down the servant's staircase and into the kitchen. It was too much to think about. The very thing that consumed her thoughts, night and day.

But with Rose leading her to freedom. She wouldn't make it on her own.

As she stood in the kitchen, trying to calm her racing heart, the room came into focus. It was a mess. Food from the last two fêtes was piled all over the counters, and there were already signs that pests were beginning to partake.

Not that Cosette didn't often leave a few crumbs on purpose for the resident mice. But just a few, and always on the floor. But she certainly didn't leave things lying about and uncovered to invite pests to move in.

It would be the first thing she cleaned up when she returned.

She grabbed the water buckets and yoke she'd made to rest upon her shoulders—very much like one used to plow fields—and was out the door and across the yard before Stasie's footsteps made it down the staircase behind her.

She needed water, and she needed it now.

14

THE WELL

osette ran through the woods, her bare feet missing every stone and branch that would cause pain, each step cushioned in a way she assumed was normal.

As she ran, small animals skipped through the forest alongside her as birds sailed through the trees from branch to branch, flitting through the air nearby and singing to her.

Hurry, hurry, hurry.

They didn't know why she was running, just that they wanted to encourage her, as they always did.

She at least knew this wasn't normal for others, so she kept this particular friendship to herself.

Even from Rosette.

She made it to the well in record time and guzzled water as she'd never done. She never wanted to be locked in her room again! But how to prevent it?

Determination swept over her. She simply must make the old woman take back her gift. After she warned her about her stepsisters.

Cosette took a moment to catch her breath, then called for the old woman. Over and over.

But she never came.

Cosette dipped out water and stayed as late as she dared, but the sun was starting to dip below the horizon, and surely her stepsisters would need help getting ready for the ball soon.

Cosette tried one last time. "S'il vous plaît, I must speak with you! My stepsisters are coming, but you must promise you won't harm them. Please!"

But still no answer came.

Shoulders slumped, Cosette lifted her burden and started back. Some boon the old woman had promised her.

Then a thought struck her heart, and she stood stock-still. What of her stepmère? She would've already discovered Cosette was missing, perhaps thought she wasn't coming back, with how long she'd been gone. She would blame Stasie.

Cosette broke out in a dead sprint, water buckets jostling on her shoulders and soaking her dress, and ran for the Comtesse's château as fast as her feet would take her.

15

SHE CAME BACK?

She came back to Stasie crying, Druce sullen with arms crossed, and Madame Béatrice in a cold fury.

"What do you mean you don't know where she is? You were supposed to go *with* her, you imbecile. How else will you find out where the well is?"

The Comtesse raised the back of her hand.

Cosette gasped and jumped forward, the mostly empty buckets sloshing noisily.

"I'm here, Stepmère."

Jewels fell into the little pouch around her neck. A few fell to the floor. Cosette reached up and adjusted the ridiculous thing that had shifted while running.

No need to give her stepmère *more* to be upset with her over.

All three women froze, staring at her.

Druce's mouth fell open a little, and Stasie's wide eyes screamed, "You came back? *Why?*"

It was the very thing Cosette was asking herself.

However, she lived in a society where females were dependent upon their pères—or in this case, her stepmère—until a husband took over the role of guardian. Striking out on one's own just wasn't done, no matter how much Cosette might wish to be free.

She had no idea how Rose had found the courage to do so, and as much as she envied that choice, it scared her half to death.

And a part of her wondered if she hadn't been intending to return from the well, if she would've even been able to go in the first place.

She gestured to the water buckets over her shoulders, hoping they wouldn't notice how much had spilled in her haste. "I brought water for you to wash up with before the ball."

Madame Béatrice didn't seem to know how to reply. "Yes, well, very good. Take it to the kitchen, then fill our water basins."

Stasie and Druce slinked away while their mère was distracted, and Cosette bobbed a curtsey with rather quite a lot of effort.

"Shall I bring you something to drink as well, Stepmère?"

Her mouth parted in surprise, but she covered it quickly. "Need you ask? And don't dawdle. The sun is starting its descent. I'll not be late because of *you*."

The Comtesse hurried over, picked up the few pearls that had fallen to the floor, then dumped the pouch in her hand.

She eyed Cosette suspiciously, then swept up her skirts and hastened away, not even noticing her twins were no longer present. Or not caring.

Which was fine by Cosette.

She breathed a sigh of relief that she'd stopped yet another disaster, pulled her soaked dress away from her freezing skin, and hurried to the kitchen.

Hopefully she'd kept enough water in the buckets to see to their needs tonight.

But first—she needed to find her change of clothes.

16

HER MÈRE'S DRESSES

Cosette made herself scarce, letting them help each other get ready, shying into another part of the house each time someone tried to seek her out for help.

Her stepsisters let her be.

Until it was time for them to go, and raised voices came to her from the hallway.

"Ouch! Watch where you shove that pin, stupid bête!" Madame Béatrice snapped.

A sharp slap, and Stasie cried out. Druce sucked in a gust of breath, a startled sound.

Cosette tumbled to a halt on her way to another part of the house. She took a deep breath and moved to join them in the front hallway.

If she were present, her stepmère's ire would be directed at her, not them. Hopefully.

She rounded the corner and froze.

Each was richly attired in heavy brocade, skirts full, barely altered from the exquisite gowns they had been before. Just enough to fit their vastly different frames.

Her mère's dresses on them. On them! She'd been taken

advantage of, her treasure stolen, just so these, these *cows* could wear what was most precious to her?

Why hadn't the seamstress sold the fabric to someone else? Anyone else? Why did it have to be *them*?

"Ah, there you are."

Her stepmère's thunderclap of harsh words broke her utter horror.

"Come now. We must take you upstairs before the carriage gets here, non?"

The Comtesse came toward her with swift steps, searching again for the right key on her keyring.

But before she could grab Cosette, herd her up the stairs, and back into her prison, Cosette darted around her and out the front door.

"What—where do you think you're going, young lady? Come ba—"

Her stepmère's words were interrupted with a crash Cosette didn't bother to investigate.

She didn't stop running, not until the forest had swallowed her whole.

17

COSETTE RUNS AWAY

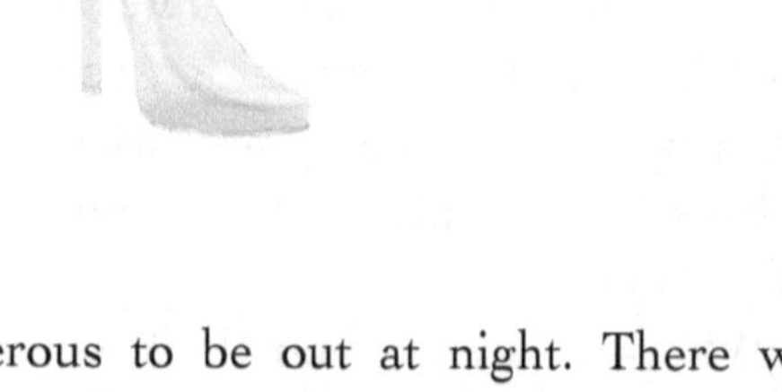

It was dangerous to be out at night. There were wolves. Wolves that ate people. Wolves that had no problem walking right into town and dragging off a small child. Or converging upon a full-grown man and taking him down.

Cosette knew that, but she kept going.

Right up to the farthest boundary line on their estate, where she could go no further.

Jaw clenched, she tried to push past it this time, but blinding pain arced through her body, sending her stumbling back, gasping for breath.

The pain immediately snuffed out when she was safely back within the property.

She stared into the dark woods, eyes wide, chest heaving with breaths.

What could it possibly mean? She could not *physically* disobey her père's words? Or was it her own words that had condemned her?

Distant howls sent chills skittering over her skin and down her spine, and she spun toward the sound, ready to flee.

Just not toward the house.

Better wolves than being locked away for yet another night, wasting yet another opportunity to find out what had happened to her sister.

Wasting another chance to speak to Gautier.

Cosette huddled in a paltry hiding spot, a collection of vines, dead bushes, and a scraggly tree next to the stone fence that created a bubble of space, knowing she'd be found if they sent out a search party. But surely even her stepmère couldn't spin a satisfactory tale of Cosette's bedraggled state in so little time.

Plus they would miss their precious ball.

Thankfully, the carriage came and took her stepfamily away, long after Cosette had given up hope that they'd stop calling for her.

Cosette crawled from her hiding spot and started toward the house, then looked down at herself. What to do about her filth?

She'd been locked up for far too long, and she was still thirsty, lightheaded, and beyond hungry. Surely they'd used up the meager amount of water she'd brought from the well.

She crept into the kitchen, determined to find a way to cleanse herself and get back to the ball.

The food mess was still out, still attracting flies and other pests, but Cosette fell upon it like it was manna straight from heaven. Most of it stuck to the roof of her mouth, too dry to go down. She needed water. Desperately.

If her stepmère kept her locked up every night—as she was sure to do now that Cosette had openly defied her—this might be Cosette's only chance to talk to Gautier.

How to get in? She only had the one dress, surely recognizable, even if Cosette had the heart to try to alter it again. Her stepmère would be on high alert. Perhaps notify the guards about some threat to Gautier.

Cosette sneaked into the rest of the house, going for her hidden dress and shoes, stopping to see if her stepfamily's washbasins held any remaining water. Telling herself she'd only guzzle it down if it wasn't too dirty.

Stasie and Druce had both left a little water in the bottom of their cups, on their nightstands, but all three washbasins had been dumped out the window.

As if to further deter her from going.

Cosette guzzled one, then made herself save the other to clean up with.

She did the best she could with one damp washrag, then did her best with the dress.

She was too tired, too heartsore, to do much, and the dress didn't want to stray far from what it had been created to be, from what she'd once made it to be.

Still she put everything she had into it, everything she could do to make the dress more than it was.

Very little changed.

Sighing, she put it on, colors awhirl, fabric rougher than before, then slipped on the shoes. She tucked the pouch into the front of her dress, where she could cover it and her mouth with a fan anytime she needed to speak, and wished for her masque.

Not that it had done much good the first time.

Yet she couldn't help the excitement that beat in her chest. She knew *they* would be watching for her. She knew she may be unable to get close to Gautier. She knew this was a fool's errand, her wishes no more than a dream.

Yet her heart took flight anyway.

18

FÉE MARRAINE

Cosette was sneaking away when the woman spoke and scared her partway to her grave.

"You didn't come to me for help."

Cosette yelped and spun around. The old woman from the forest stood there, in the same rags but standing taller than before, perhaps with fewer wrinkles, and watched her with a cool look.

"Why is that?"

Cosette's mouth hung open far too long before she snapped it closed. She didn't know what to say. "I—I— Forgive me, Madame."

Cosette dipped a curtsey, not wanting to get on the woman's bad side, not with the things she could do, and waited for her response.

Yet her eyes drifted toward the château where the ball was being held, and she couldn't help a trickle of impatience that she'd rather be dancing right now.

Getting closer to Gautier.

The woman eyed the little pouch the gems fell in and muttered, "Clever." Louder, she said, "You should learn to use your connections when you most need them, chérie."

Mind spinning, Cosette didn't know what to say to that. She had called her. Many times. At the well. She just hadn't thought of it this time.

The woman looked Cosette's dress over, all the way down to her shoes. Her gaze lingered there. "Although I must say you didn't do too badly at all."

Pleasure flushed through Cosette, but she dipped her head so the fey creature wouldn't see her worry.

She didn't have much hope that the dress would last the night. She was weary, and the part of her that, even unconsciously, wanted to make sure her stepsisters knew how much the gift meant to her, wouldn't let the dress transform completely.

Though she didn't know that.

She honestly didn't know why this dress wouldn't keep the changes that stuck to every other article of clothing she improved.

"Those shoes . . ." Suddenly, the woman's gaze darted to the trees, and every glowbug within sight fled, deep into the forest. "Hmm. I see."

Cosette couldn't tell if the woman was pleased or upset or felt nothing at all. She tried to smooth things over, just in case. "The shoes were the loveliest gift, thank you." She swished her skirts and pointed a toe. "I've never owned anything more beautiful in my life."

The woman looked slightly mollified, but her words were still somewhat clipped. "Were you planning on walking the whole way?"

Shrugging, Cosette tried to pretend it didn't bother her. "I really have no other choice." She bit her lip. "Though I hate the thought of causing offense. I'm so very late as it is."

A hint of a smile peeked through. "Don't you worry about that, my dear. The minute you walk in, no one will be able to take their eyes off you."

Cosette ducked her head and blushed furiously.

"But we can't let you walk all the way to the ball, now can we?"

Cosette opened her mouth—to say what, she didn't know —but before she could, the woman snapped her fingers, and the glowbugs came racing back. Hundreds of them.

"My carriage. Horses. Eight, I think. Coachman. Footman. Now."

The shining insects converged and raced away in a panic, like stardust exploding, fluttering in a mad race everywhere all at once, as if too flustered to obey her commands.

Cosette squinted, trying to see what they really were, but just as before, she couldn't make anything out past the light they gave off.

They rushed around, doing who knows what, until they converged once more and formed a carriage outline made of glowing lights, on the other side of the garden.

Cosette took a step back. Everything the woman had ordered was outlined in glowing lights, the carriage, the horses, the two men, everything.

"You'll need it solid, won't you? Of course you will."

The fey woman snapped her fingers, and a hum started, grew louder, then cut out suddenly. The lights winked out.

Across from her stood a white carriage enhanced with gold, glass, and diamonds, along with eight strong white horses, a stoic-looking coachman, and a reserved-looking footman.

She couldn't help it—she gasped and nearly fell into the bushes.

"Footman?" the fairy called.

Cosette nearly jumped out of her skin when he stood just next to them—not at the carriage where he'd been, mere moments before—waiting on his mistress's commands. He was dressed in gold cloth with silver embellishments and diamonds as his buttons.

"Ah. There you are. Prepare my carriage for the young Mademoiselle, s'il vous plaît?"

He bowed, then poofed out of existence.

"Coachman?" He looked up from where he was sitting at the front of the carriage. "Bring it around, will you?"

"Wha — ?" Cosette couldn't manage to ask.

But the creak of carriage wheels interrupted her.

The pure-white carriage — so white it looked as if it were made from her mère's fine bone porcelain, and just as delicate — came rumbling toward her, across the garden, through the chicken coup, and straight up to the boundary of their property, near the back stone fence, where she'd been sneaking over for the most direct route to the château.

If it would let her this time, as it had the first time she'd gone to the ball.

The carriage didn't touch anything it rumbled through or across, leaving everything just as it had been.

Cosette let out the breath she'd been holding. At least that was one mess she wouldn't be coming back to.

It circled her once then came to a stop before her, as if putting itself on display. Every accent was gilded gold in every place imaginable. The pure-white horses even had pure-gold harnesses.

And yet . . . . the white was a little too white. The gold a little too vibrant. The carriage creaked and groaned in such a way that sounded like it was *trying* to sound like a real carriage, but was somehow . . . off.

Had Cosette gone completely mad? Or had crying so much made the whole world seem more than it was?

The footman opened the door for her, revealing plush velvet cushions, and held one hand out for her to take, inviting her to step within and be whisked away.

"Now be good to my servants, you hear? You have only till the sun rises in the east, and if you're not back by then — well, just you be back by then."

Cosette was having trouble taking it all in. "Why until the sun rises?"

The fairy-witch offered Cosette a wan smile. "You let me worry about that. You worry about having a lovely time."

Cosette didn't know how to thank her. It could never be enough.

And the old woman still looked bothered. "Why didn't you ask me for help? It was a simple enough thing."

Cosette almost demurred again, almost put the blame on herself or deflected what had happened, but she was too overcome, too frazzled, too heartsore, to keep the truth from spilling out.

"I did! I called and called for you—but you never came."

The old woman eyed her speculatively, almost as if she didn't believe her . . . well, exactly like that.

One of the glowbugs came right up to her and hovered over her shoulder. She seemed to be listening to whatever it was saying.

Though Cosette couldn't hear a thing.

"Ah. I see." The glowbug flitted off, and the woman's attention rested solely on Cosette. "You must ask me for yourself. Not for others."

Cosette's mouth fell open. That went against everything she believed! Everything she was taught in Mass, at her mère's knee, from society.

Put others before yourself. Don't make a fuss. Meet others' needs readily and willingly and silently, if at all possible.

It was her place.

The woman continued. "I can't hear you, otherwise." Taking in the look on Cosette's face, she came close and gently cupped Cosette's chin in her hand. "Ma chère, I offered *you* a boon, not someone else."

Cosette lifted her chin. The motion didn't dislodge the woman's hand. "What if I want to use it for someone else?"

She smiled gently. "That's not how it works."

It didn't make sense why this woman would do that. All of this. For her. For a simple drink of water.

"Who are you?" she whispered. Three pearls fell into the pouch.

The woman laughed and spread her hands wide, taking a step back, as if showing herself off. "Have you not guessed it, ma chère? I am your Fée Marraine!"

Her fairy godmother? Cosette gasped, overcome for a moment that such things from the fairy tales existed in real life, then tilted her head.

The words sounded false. Like Cosette's did, when she purposefully left out information or adjusted them just so to lead the hearer in another direction—the only way she'd been able to keep the truth from spilling out of her lips, especially when it might harm someone else.

Then it was all too much.

Heartache welled and came spilling out.

Cosette flung herself at the woman's feet, grasped her skirts, and begged. "Please, please, I beg of you! Take this curse from me! No more gems. No more pearls. I don't want it. I beg of you—I don't want it!"

More gems spilled out of her mouth, as they had been the whole conversation, some into the pouch, most onto the ground.

The woman sniffed. "Not a very nice way to treat a gift. And calling it a curse? Hardly, my dear. Why would I take it back?"

Cosette wailed and buried her face in the woman's skirts.

"My, my, but your human side is dramatic, isn't it? There, there, child. Let go of my skirts. All will be well."

The voluminous black material was wrested from Cosette's grasp, and she slumped to the ground and covered her face. How could she tell the old woman what her cursed gift had brought on Cosette? It was too humiliating to say aloud.

And who would believe such a tale?

Cosette wouldn't have. Not until it had been done to her.

"Oh!"

Cosette looked up. The woman's face had brightened.

"You want to talk to your friends at the fête without drowning them in jewels, is that it?"

Cosette hesitated, but the woman looked so eager, Cosette finally nodded.

True, but not the entire truth.

She patted Cosette's cheek, then wiped away a few tears with her thumb. "Well then, that's perfectly understandable, my dear. What say you we add a little pause on your gift while you wear your shoes? How's that?"

Cosette nodded again, feeling utterly hopeless, not knowing what else to say. How else to get the Fée Marraine to listen to her?

Her stepmère, long before she'd started showing her true self, had once emphasized that their family business was private and not to be gossiped about to those outside their immediate family.

When asked if she'd ever do such a thing, Cosette had given an indignant "of course not," and with that, her lips had been sealed.

She could tell no one but her immediate family—of which she was firmly including Rose—of what her stepmère did or said to them all.

But she hadn't realized it until this very moment.

If only Rose were here to speak up on Cosette's behalf.

The fairy godmère gave Cosette's cheek a final pat. "Then you'll find the jewels on your pillow when you return."

Cosette bolted upright, horror flooding her. "Non, please!"

The woman tisked. "Let's not be overly dramatic, my dear. Of course you'll want the jewels." She eyed Cosette's dress. "Do be sure to save some for your needs in the future. I understand wanting to spend them all on frivolities after so long without, but there are still many hard days ahead, to be sure."

Mouth falling open, Cosette couldn't even fathom a response.

"But enough of that!" The woman hauled Cosette to her feet and brushed her off. "It's time you were off."

Perhaps . . . there was one way to be heard. One way to get the fairy to listen.

The control Cosette held over her dress slipped, and the scraps it had been sewn from blossomed back. She deliberately released the illusion of before, the soft, silky material, the pastel swirl of colors, the smooth stitches and hems.

Cosette swished the material, but the fey didn't seem to notice, her attention elsewhere.

"But please . . . my dress . . ."

The fairy took a closer look at the dress. Then pursed her lips.

Cosette was still holding on to . . . something. The old woman couldn't see it as it truly was.

Perhaps she was still clinging to the kindness with which her stepsisters had made the garment. The idea that they'd thought of her with every stitch.

She was still clinging to it for their sake, not her own.

Too weary to keep it any longer, Cosette let go of her hold entirely, and the monstrosity her stepsisters had made in a brief fit of kindness made itself fully known.

Her Fée Marraine gasped and staggered back a step. "Ma chère, you simply cannot go to the fête in *that*!"

Cosette gave her a small, innocent smile.

She looked between the dress and Cosette, before apparently deciding not to bring up the fact that the dress hadn't been this awful mere seconds ago.

Carefully choosing each word, Cosette tried to come up with the right thing to say to show this woman that her gift was not as delightful as it seemed. That she needed to take it *back*.

But her Fée Marraine was solely focused on the problem before her. "Let's see . . . shall we make it in the old style, the elegant style, in pink—"

"My favorite color is blue," Cosette blurted.

It couldn't be like her mère's dress. She was too close to the heartache. She wasn't ready.

"In blue," the woman corrected, not missing a beat. "With lace spilling from three-quarter sleeves, layers enough to make even the queen happy—"

Cosette's heart gave a pang at the mention of the missing ruler.

"—and skirts so voluminous that any gentleman who wishes to dance with you or take you into his arms will need to do battle to get anywhere near you."

She had a gleeful look in her eyes, quite like a matchmaker.

Or perhaps someone who liked lace far more than was good for her.

Cosette laughed, the sound still wet from her recent tears, but she almost rolled her eyes too.

An unfortunate habit she'd picked up from her sister.

She wasn't going to the ball to be matched to anyone—she was going to find out what had happened to Rose. Nothing more.

As the woman spoke, the glowbugs converged upon Cosette, sweeping her up into blinding, glittering lights, then all fled at once into the trees.

She was no longer wearing a simple day dress.

Non, a baby-blue skirt and stomacher, stitched with flowers, dandelions in particular, peeked out from under the navy-blue outer skirt and jacket. A mantle swept from her shoulders to the ground, sewn into the outer dress itself.

Lace spilled from every hem imaginable, and crushed-silk

poofs the size of thimbles lined every edge, keeping with the dandelion theme.

Cosette had a brief flash of concern that she might not fit into the carriage.

Then the fairy godmère placed a glittering crown atop Cosette's head, nestled among the curls now piled there and spilling over her shoulders. "There, the perfect touch."

"Oh!" said Cosette. "But I am not royalty. I couldn't possibly."

"Tonight you are," said the older woman. "A princess from a far-off land. And don't you forget it."

Cosette couldn't argue with her.

She looked like the nobility of old. Like royalty.

And she didn't mind one bit.

She spun, taking in as much of the dress as possible.

"Oh, merci, Fée Marraine, merci!"

"There, there. No thanks necessary."

Cosette couldn't agree. She deserved so much gratitude and more! Who had blessed her with a fairy godmother? Had her mère truly known the fey? Why had she never met the woman before?

"One more thing." The fairy came over and kissed Cosette's forehead. She gave her a warm smile. "Now they won't recognize you."

A golden masque fitted itself to her face, and Cosette reached up and touched it. "Because of the masque?"

Because that had failed her in the past.

"Non, because of my kiss." She shrugged in a very French-like manner. "Though the masque will help, bien sûr."

Too stunned to do anything but gape, Cosette stared up at the taller woman in awe.

A little of her aloofness trickled back in, and the fairy stepped back. "Off with you now. Those slippers won't dance by themselves!"

Cosette threw her arms around the woman, squeezed her tight, then raced for the carriage.

The footman bustled her inside, and soon she was looking out the window at the woman who had turned her world upside down, inside out, and not even a little the same as before.

As the carriage jerked forward, she called after Cosette, "Not a moment after the sun touches the horizon, you hear? Your life depends upon it!"

Cosette waved to show she'd heard, then she took to inspecting every inch of the carriage as it took off down the road, so fast it felt like flying.

She looked up just as they hurtled past the front gate.

Cosette yelped, but not even a tingle of pain touched her. Perhaps because she wasn't running away? Or because she was in the fairy's carriage?

She would love to know.

But first, she was going to enjoy every moment of this exquisite evening.

So of course she stuck her head out the window, closed her eyes, and enjoyed the delicious feel of the wind in her hair and the cool breeze upon her face.

Hopefully the curls piled high and spilling down her shoulders wouldn't be too tousled.

They arrived at the château almost too soon.

19

A MAGICAL BALL

Adjusting the masque yet one more time, Cosette's hands shook as her carriage came to rest before the château's entrance.

Should she really be here? What would happen to her if her stepmère found out? Was she truly hidden from being recognized, merely from a fairy's kiss?

She certainly hoped so.

Then the footman was upon her, and she didn't have a moment further to worry or wring her hands.

Cosette alighted from the carriage, one regal step after another, and she clung to the footman's hand just a little harder than she meant to.

"Don't you worry a whit, Mademoiselle," he said quietly. "They won't be able to take their eyes off you."

Offering him a trembling smile, she took a deep breath, nodded, and forced herself to release his hand.

She was here to see Gautier, and she had to act as if she belonged.

Which in another world, she would have.

She was later than the other guests, but the old woman—

and the footman—had been right. Conversation hushed as she passed. All eyes turned toward her.

Fey magic was irresistible to humans, Cosette knew this, but she couldn't help the little thrill that went through her at all the attention. It was as if she'd put on another persona, one she was far more comfortable with, and was in her element for the first time in her life.

Cosette walked into the fête in a daze. The small château was polished to a blazing shine, its gilding touched up, garlands strung everywhere. Candles lit the space with a warm golden glow, and Cosette felt right at home.

She spun in a slow circle, taking everything in.

It was even more glorious than the last time she'd been here.

Then she'd been overcome, overwhelmed, and deliriously happy, and the night had passed in a blur.

Now it seemed as if everyone had settled into a rhythm, no longer mobbing, no longer desperate for something they'd been without for so long.

This was France from before the curse. When she and Rosette would hide at the top of the stairs, faces pressed to the banister, watching vibrant colors mix and swirl as the dancers whirled and whirled and whirled around their parents' ballroom.

Cosette couldn't wait for her turn, then it was taken from her. But here she was, now—a small restoration of her hopes and dreams.

Warmth filled her. If this was even a taste of what Gautier could do while a curse still raged, wolves still attacked, food wouldn't grow, and winter seemed to cling to everything— maybe Rosette was wrong about him.

The thought of her sister, the whole reason for her being here, jolted her back into motion.

She swept through the foyer, heading straight for the double doors from whence music and joyous laughter spilled.

When she glided into the ballroom itself, conversation abruptly ceased.

The marquis's herald held out his hand for her card, and Cosette panicked for half a second. Then she remembered who she was, why she had to be here, and gave him her most winsome smile.

And threw out the first name she could think of.

"Cendrillon, princess from a far-off land, to present herself to Monsieur Gautier."

After all, her Fée Marraine had put the idea in her head.

And her stepsisters made fun of her often enough for how covered in ashes she became every time she cleaned out the fireplaces.

Astonishingly, the words didn't taste like a lie on her tongue.

In fact, she halfway felt she'd known a Cendrillon once . . . but a princess?

Now she had even more questions. Perhaps her disguise had allowed her to say the words?

She would have to find a way to ask her Fée Marraine.

The herald repeated her, word for word, then escorted her before the hosts of the ball themselves, the Marquis and Marquise Montagne, who had been standing on the balcony overlooking the ballroom, watching the revelers with smiles on their faces.

They looked hardly able to contain themselves—or utter coherent responses—to hosting royalty.

Cosette dipped into a curtsey, careful not to make it too deep, as befitted her supposed station, and rose with the same elegance.

Disappointment crashed through her that Gautier wasn't in the reception line with his hosts. Would she be able to find him? Speak to him? Dance with him?

Her eyes discreetly swept the room, but he was nowhere in sight.

Once the hosts had acknowledged her, a man's shoes tapped the floor in a rapid, echoing staccato as he came toward her swiftly. Rather tall, handsome, and blessed with a stunning smile, he wore a red frock coat with shining brass buttons.

Gleaming white teeth shone at her from behind his mask.

Cosette fluttered her fan as he bowed.

"May I have the honor of this dance, Mademoiselle?"

She glanced at her hosts—it was Monsieur Montagne's right to dance with her first if he so pleased—but he smiled and swept out his arm, as if giving them his blessing.

Cosette daintily laid her hand upon the man's outstretched one. "It would be my honor."

He took her fingertips and led her down onto the dance floor, arm fully extended as if he were simultaneously showing her off while not engulfing himself in her voluminous skirts.

Every eye was upon them, and whispers swirled after them like a gentle wind.

He swept her out onto the floor, the music began, and Cosette lost herself to pure, unadulterated bliss.

20

DANCING ALL NIGHT

Cosette must have danced with every man present, but she danced most often with the one who had asked her first. And she hadn't even caught his name.

"Where did you come from?" the man asked in a daze, staring at her like he wanted to gobble her all up.

Cosette couldn't decide if it was flattering or concerning, but she just smiled and answered vaguely, "Oh, from a land of mist and sunshine where happiness dwells and kindness is never forgotten."

She often dreamed of such a place.

The man laughed like her wit astounded him, then said, "No, really. Who are you? Where did you come from? How did you . . . get in, with the borders to the country closed?"

"Oh! Oh, you see, I'm not from *that* far away." She flushed. She hadn't meant for that to be inferred from what she'd said.

He continued to stare at her as they swept in and around other couples in intricate dance steps.

Cosette met his eyes, surprised to find they were intent, serious. Still waiting. So she gave him a direct answer. "I am here to meet Gautier." She shrugged, trying to seem nonchalant. "I wish to speak with him about a most delicate matter."

The man looked stunned for three beats. "Gautier . . . to speak with him."

Cosette nodded prettily, then let her gaze wander, lest he think her too interested. "I heard he would be here, and I hoped he would take a moment for me. To answer my questions."

"And you . . . have not danced with him yet?"

"Surely he will ask me at some point," she mused, trying not to be too put out that he hadn't.

According to the bit of gossip she'd gleaned, he met the guests in the reception line, which Cosette had been too late to be a part of, opened the ball for dancing, then vanished until he closed the fête with some grand announcement.

Much like the first time she'd come, except for the part about his disappearing.

Apparently he didn't like to be mobbed all evening by adoring crowds.

Not that Cosette blamed him.

"And if you met him, this Gautier, what would you say to him?"

She laughed. "Now that is for him to hear, is it not?"

"You know what he looks like, do you?" the man asked carefully.

"Oh, I haven't met him. Only heard of him," she clarified, looking past his shoulder. Which she sincerely hoped to rectify soon. "But I believe I will recognize him when I see him."

The man threw back his head and laughed.

Cosette missed a step and spun on him, startled. "What— did I say something humorous, Monsieur?"

"Forgive me. I could not help myself." His eyes danced with mirth, and his ever-on-display teeth flashed in the candlelight. "You see, I may be able to—"

At that moment, the orchestra ended with a flourish, couples parted to clap and cheer and generally make conversation impossible, and a mob of young Monsieurs swarmed Cosette for her next dance.

She laughed and fluttered her fan—which was a shade of pink that most certainly must have been a small rebellion from her Fée Marraine—and agreed to as many dances as she could hope for and more. She only wished she had a dance card to keep them all straight.

Then she was swept into the next song, and the urgency of finding Gautier faded, just a little.

It had been so long—what could a few dances hurt?

21

FLY SWIFT AND TRUE

Cosette stood next to the punch bowl and guzzled, trying to be demure with so many eyes upon her, but she'd hardly stopped dancing since she'd come in.

As she nodded at the young man prattling at her side and offered her cup for a refill, Cosette couldn't help but notice that many women besides her stepfamily wore new dresses.

The town dressmaker stood to the side, her ombre skin gleaming in the candlelight, beaming at her and her girls' handiwork, accomplished in so little time.

And showing off the lovely gowns they themselves wore, of course.

A new appreciation for Gautier swelled in Cosette. To give that woman, the dressmaker, the dignity of running her own shop again, and then invite her and her shop girls to the same ball—maybe France would see an end to this curse's hardship under such a leader.

Maybe Rose was wrong about him. Maybe Gautier *was* doing good for his country. He had hired huntsmen—and one huntswoman, the best of them all, in Cosette's humble opinion—to kill the wolves attacking his people, hadn't he?

She simply had to meet him and decide for herself.

93

Which was the whole reason she was here in the first place.

She disentangled herself from the young man with a smile and a non-answer about giving him yet another dance, then went in search of her hosts.

Surely they could point her in the right direction.

Music swelled and another dance went into full swing, so she veered to the side and slipped along the wall to stay out of the crush as much as possible.

Strange, in all the times Rose had talked to her about him, she'd never once described what Gautier looked like.

Then again, Cosette had always been fascinated by people, watching them, getting to know them, helping them, while Rose tended to avoid others as much as humanly possible.

Why hadn't she made more of an effort to get close to him the first night she'd come, to get a good look at him?

No matter. Her hosts would know.

But they could not be found.

Had they retired with Gautier, to come out only once the final announcement of the evening was upon them?

She didn't know, but before she could find out, there he was again, the man who simply could not get enough of her, hand held out. "May I implore you for yet one more dance, fair Mademoiselle?"

Cosette laughed and fluttered her fan, trying not to be obvious as she looked past him. "Surely others would cast you as my favorite, were I to do so."

He leaned close and gave her a piercing look, one corner of his mouth tilted up. "Would they be wrong?"

She couldn't help her flush, so she swept her fan harder. Had all the air just been sucked out of the room?

The man smiled and withdrew a little, visibly pleased by her reaction. "It's the last dance of the ball, Mademoiselle. Surely you can—"

Whatever else he was about to say was lost as Cosette

spun toward the floor-to-ceiling windows at the back of the ballroom, two doors on either side open to let cool air into the stifling ballroom and to lead overheated guests into the coolness of the garden.

But neither the glass nor the open doors showed any lightness to the sky.

"I do not know, Monsieur," she mumbled, biting her lip. "I did not realize it was so late."

He gently pulled her to the dance floor. "I'm afraid I cannot accept a refusal," he said lightly. "I simply must find out who you are before this night is over and you are lost to me."

Cosette looked up at him with wide eyes. The words were a little too possessive for her liking.

"You will be back tomorrow night, will you not?" he asked, already guiding her through the dance with warm, gentle hands.

She gave in to the familiar steps, fluttering her fan with one hand to cover her unease. "That is my plan, oui. I have not yet met Gautier, after all."

He beamed at her. "Brilliant."

The music was coming to a close when the ballgoers took up the chant, "Speech, speech, speech!"

Cosette turned toward where they were all looking, the balcony, and said, "Speech?"

He released her hand, yet stayed as close to her as he could get. Cosette found herself grateful for the wide skirts and all their layers. She didn't know what she thought of this gentleman yet, of his familiarity with her, but she was thankful for the distance while she made up her mind.

"Ah, yes. It would appear the people are eager for their prince to give his nightly speech, to end the evening."

She spun on him and demanded, "Prince?"

He looked rather uncomfortable.

Then the name "Gautier" came through the chant next.

"Gautier is posturing himself as the people's prince? What of the royal family? What if when the curse is broken, they come back?"

The man with the brass buttons laughed, though it was decidedly strained. "No one wishes to find the royal family more than Gautier, I assure you, but we must move forward. The prince cannot be found, so Gautier must do the best he can in the royal family's absence."

Cosette was aghast. "But he is not the prince. He is not part of the royal family. His father was only a steward, therefore he could not possibly—"

The man cut her off, more strain to his voice than was warranted. "He has only the best of intentions. Who better to lead the country than the one person who has stayed, the one person who has bled, agonized, spent every waking moment trying to make his people's lives better? I, for one, will support him fully should the people award him the throne."

Cosette nodded, ashamed of herself, hardly daring to look at him. If only she could escape this most awkward of conversations. What was it about him that flustered her so? "You are right, of course. Forgive me."

"There is nothing to forgive." He pulled her closer as the chant grew louder. "Please, Mademoiselle. I must go. Your name? Your father's name, perhaps? I simply must—"

The crush jostled them apart as people pressed toward the balcony, eager for whatever Gautier had to say. Cosette used the distraction to make her escape.

It wasn't until she was in the garden, shaking, that she realized how light the sky had actually become.

Her Fée Marraine's warning echoed in her head.

She didn't know what the consequences would be were she to be here when the sun breached the horizon, but she wasn't keen on finding out.

She would simply have to return tomorrow night and not

stop looking until she found him. Until she found out what he knew about her sister.

Cosette escaped the garden, ran across the wide expanse of the château's grounds, and deep into the forest, intent on getting home before her stepfamily.

22

DAYDREAMS OF A BALL

Cosette ran the entire way back. She felt as if her feet had wings, and her dress flowed around her in a rustle of loveliness that lifted her above her tiredness.

After she'd hurried into the kitchen, the dress melted back into rags the moment the sun touched the horizon.

She ran to the servant's quarters, hid her dress and shoes, and bolted for the kitchen.

She'd cut it too close. She'd been so enraptured, so enjoying the attention, so intent on meeting Gautier, she hadn't paid attention to the time.

She stopped. Or the fact that she had a perfectly good carriage she could've used to get back even faster.

She groaned and kept going.

Thank goodness whatever her Fée Marraine warned her of hadn't happened.

She rolled the thin mattress off her bed and hauled it in front of the fireplace. No way was she giving her stepfamily a door to lock her behind.

Thankfully there were still coals. She swirled the ash and blew on the embers to glow hotter.

Harnesses rattled and horses' hooves clomped up the

98

drive, so she grabbed a handful of cool ash and smeared it on her face, the backs of her hands, and on her apron.

Then she pulled the threadbare blanket over her shoulders, lay down, and huddled close to the open fireplace as if she were cold. It was all she could do to pretend to sleep while her stepfamily ransacked the house, looking for her.

Footsteps. On the steps leading down into the kitchen.

"Maman! She is here!" Druce shrieked, not even trying to be a little quiet.

Cosette held perfectly still.

The other two women rushed into the kitchen. All three crowded around her.

"Is she dead?" Stase asked fearfully.

"Don't be ridiculous," Druce shot back.

But they all leaned a little closer.

Cosette sincerely hoped she wouldn't shiver and give her sleepless self away. But it was cold on the floor, and her nerves were tangling her stomach into knots.

Someone poked her.

She turned her gasp into a yawn, then blearily looked around, focusing on the women above her after a moment. "Oh! Are you back? How was the fête?"

Gems spilled onto the pillow by her head.

A pang lit up her heart. She had so loved not having the reminder of her stepmère's greed.

She yawned and stretched, then pulled the blanket up higher and curled into a ball, as if to go back to sleep.

The sun was just slipping awake, after all, and she hadn't yet been to bed.

Not that she'd be able to sleep with their watching her.

"Where have you been all night? Where did you go when you ran away?" her stepmère demanded.

Cosette answered sleepily, "Well, first I went for a walk, then I got lost in the dark"—true, but only briefly on the way home—"and I was never more thankful to find warm coals and a mattress to rest my head."

Almost true. She *was* thankful for the coals and mattress. Too bad they were both *here*.

"Nothing else? Nowhere else?"

Cosette stretched and yawned and made a noncommittal noise, not daring to answer.

"Maman, look at her. Covered in soot and ash," Stasie said.

"And grubby to boot." The sneer in Druce's voice was unmistakable. "Remnants of the forest all over her."

Stasie dropped her voice. "No way did she sneak out to, well, you know."

Druce laughed, the sound hard and cruel. "They wouldn't have let her in. Even the Montagnes have *some* standards for their guests."

Cosette sat up slowly, shoulders hunched, and stared into the coals. She wrapped her blanket tighter around her. "Do you want me to get your breakfast?" she whispered, just wanting the cruel words to stop.

"Well. Oui," her stepmère said. "Just . . . clean up first. Before you touch our food."

Cosette nodded, wanting them to leave with every fiber in her being. The girls gathered up the gems and handed them to their mother. Something more happened behind her, some whispering, then her stepmère left.

She looked up at her stepsisters, but Druce looked away, and Stasie shook her head.

Soon a clanking sound met her ears.

Her stepmère entered, a length of chain stretched between her hands. "Hold her."

Cosette gasped, tried to run. Got tangled up in the blanket and mattress.

Druce was quick to pounce, holding her shoulder and elbow in each hand. Stase was slower—Cosette almost threw off Druce in those precious seconds—but then Stasie had her, and her legs were still tangled in the blanket.

Madame Béatrice took out a key and fastened one manacle to Cosette's ankle, the other to the table leg.

The heavy table. That Cosette couldn't lift. Where she prepared all their meals.

"But, please! The water! I must go draw water!" Cosette begged.

The Comtesse sneered. "You'll not go anywhere until I trust you to take my girls and not run off again. Besides, the Montagne's butler was more than happy to oblige when I requested water along with our food. More than enough to last us through the ball."

Cosette choked on a sob.

Madame Béatrice beamed at her, triumphant, nose in the air. "Girls, go get the food and water left by our front door, and bring it here for Cosette to put away."

The girls looked between Cosette and their mother.

"*Us* do it?" Druce protested. "Why can't *she*—"

"Now!" she barked.

The girls scrambled away.

Cosette bit her hand to keep from crying in front of the Comtesse. Especially without anyone else here.

The girls were soon hurrying back and forth, bringing in their pillage. The heavy water barrels—small enough to be carried—were last, and the Comtesse eyed Cosette coldly.

"And don't even think about spilling them. Then you'll go without, not us. We have more upstairs. Out of *your* reach."

With that, Madame Béatrice left, leaving the girls all looking at each other.

"You just had to run off, didn't you?" Druce said the moment her mother's footsteps couldn't be heard.

"Hush, you," Stasie said, still breathing hard from carrying everything. "It's not like you wouldn't have done the same had you been in her place."

Druce crossed her arms. "I would never *be* in her place. No one is that stupid."

Stase started to protest, but Druce rolled her eyes and interrupted. "You do realize this means we'll be doing all the chores that aren't in this kitchen? Until we leave?"

Stasie snapped her mouth closed.

"Didn't think of that, did you?" She turned her sneer on Cosette. "Thanks for making extra work for us."

"Druce," Stasie feebly protested.

Cosette wouldn't look at either of them, shame running through her like an ocean current.

"Come on," Druce said. "She's not going anywhere. Let's go lay out our clothes for tonight—we'll be helping each other get ready. Again."

Cosette didn't see the disgruntled look Druce shot her, but she was certain it was there.

"Do you think we'll dance with Gautier again?"

Cosette startled and looked up.

Druce laughed and nudged her sister. "Ooh, you should've seen her face!"

Stasie gave an uneasy chuckle, but she still wouldn't look at Cosette. Then they were both heading upstairs, Druce talking loudly of the ball, the food, the dresses, and most of all: Gautier.

23

LOCKED IN

A noise sounded just outside the kitchen door, and Cosette dropped the knife she'd been using to pick at the manacle's lock.

She'd already broken its tip, but the fillet knife still seemed to reach the tumblers, though she'd had no success whatsoever getting them to turn.

Who knew this was a skill she would need one day?

Rosette probably would've had it open in ten seconds flat.

She jumped up and, with her foot, shoved the knife under the closest piece of furniture, where she usually left crumbs for the mice. Then she spun back to the meal that had been devoured by her stepfamily, crumbs left for her to clean up on their messy trays.

She'd had so little time to mess with the locks, since they checked on her so often, that it had been an agonizing day spent snatching naps before the fire, picking the lock when she wasn't being watched, and cleaning their mess while trying to pretend their watching didn't bother her.

She plunked the soapy rag onto the next dish, scrubbing like she'd been doing it all along. The water was gross and cold. She needed to reheat it. Again.

The jangle of keys tensed her shoulders up by her ears.

"You'll have to save that for tomorrow," came her step-mère's cold voice, "because it's time for us to leave." She bent and undid the manacle.

"But, Stepmère," Cosette feebly protested. "Pests and rats and bugs . . ."

"Will have their fair share tonight, thanks to you. You had plenty of time to clean this up," she said sharply, full of suspicion. "Make sure you aren't so slow tomorrow, oui? It would be a shame for you to let this all go to waste."

Cosette lowered her eyes. "Oui, Comtesse."

"Now hurry. The carriage will be here any moment, and I do not want to wait on you." The Comtesse clamped down on Cosette's shoulder, leaving the chain where it lay, and hauled her upstairs to her own bedroom.

Cosette's eyes widened when Madame Béatrice marched them toward her own closet.

Most people kept their clothes in a wardrobe, valuables in little chests upon mirrored armoires. Not her stepmère.

Always afraid of being stolen from, always mistrustful of servants—of anyone, really—she'd had an interior room walled in. No windows, no possible way for a thief to escape but back through her bedroom, this room was where she kept her numerous dresses and valuables locked away, the only key in her possession.

Panic threatened to close Cosette's throat. "Surely this is not necessary, Stepmère. The kitchen . . . the chain should be plenty . . ."

Madame Béatrice gave an elegant laugh. "You think I'll trust you after the trouble you've given me? I think not. You'll stay here while I'm away, and any jewels that fall from your mouth will be here, waiting for me when I return. Not squirreled away wherever you're hiding them."

"I haven't hidden any, you know I haven't." Cosette's voice was thick with tears.

Her stepmère just laughed and shoved her into the darkened space. "We shall see, now won't we?"

Cosette rushed toward the light, suddenly afraid of the dark, but the door closed, the lock clicked, and Cosette fell into a heap at the door, banging on it with her fists. "Stepmère, please non! Please do not keep me locked up in here!"

But her only answer was the slam of the bedroom door, another lock clicking firmly into place, then silence.

Cosette wrapped her arms around her legs, buried her face in her skirts, and sobbed.

24

A MOST DELIGHTFUL BATH

"**My** dear, why are you crying?"

Cosette's head came up to the genuinely curious look on her Fée Marraine's face. Cosette looked around her desperately. She was in the garden, curled up in a ball, in the same position she'd been in inside the closet.

With a gasp, she sat upright.

"And the better question is, why are you crying instead of getting ready for the ball?"

Cosette's tongue came undone at the annoyance in the fairy's tone. "The fête . . . my stepmère does not wish me to go . . . she locked the door . . ."

"Oh for heaven's sake. Humans and their petty jealousies. Here, dry your eyes, child. Of all the utter nonsense. But where is your dress?"

Cosette stared at her, bewildered, wondering if the creature understood the gravity of the situation—if she was annoyed with what her stepmère had done . . . or with Cosette. She honestly couldn't tell.

The fairy pulled Cosette to her feet. "Well? Off with you! We need something to work with, don't we? That drab gray

106

thing you're wearing won't do at all. Hurry! I haven't got all evening, chère."

Those last words got through to Cosette, and she turned and ran, sprinting to her hiding place, coming back swiftly with her dress and her shoes.

The dress was rags once again, but her shoes were as beautiful as they had always been.

The fairy studied Cosette's face. "Hmm . . . I think you need a little more . . . something . . . tonight. To relax you, non?" She clapped her hands, and the glowbugs swarmed to do her bidding. "A full bath, there. A screen? Non, it is more relaxing to enjoy nature to its fullest." Her voice and eyes turned stern. "But warn me the *moment* anyone comes!"

The glowbugs dispersed, and soon a full, luxurious bath sat in Cosette's dead garden, bubbles foaming out in a ridiculously lovely pile, the most delightful scents wafting on the breeze.

The glowbugs fled to the tips of the branches, lighting the entire courtyard in fairy lights, bringing an ethereal glow to the gloom of moments before.

Cosette breathed deep, taking a few steps toward it without realizing she'd done so. When was the last time she'd fully submerged herself in water? Had soft, foaming soap that didn't burn her skin or stink without herbs infusing it?

"I can give you an hour, no more."

Cosette nodded, any objections far away, and headed straight toward it.

"Well? What are you waiting for?" came her Fée Marraine's shrill voice. "Go make a perimeter!"

The glowbugs dispersed, leaving her in the kind of darkness she didn't mind. That of the night, where her eyes could adjust and she could see better than most.

She shivered as she removed her faded servant dress, then slipped into the tub as quickly as she could.

"When shall I—" Cosette started to ask, but her Fée Marraine was gone, and Cosette had the garden to herself.

Cosette smiled and scrubbed every inch of herself scarlet, then pulled in her dresses and scrubbed both of them as well. She would lay them on the wall to dry in just a moment, but for now, she leaned back and let them and herself soak, playing with the cloth with her toes, not realizing how much she'd missed such a simple pleasure.

"It is time, ma chérie."

Cosette gasped and bolted upright, blinking the sleep from her eyes. Her Fée Marraine held out a robe, and Cosette stood and slipped into it. Strange, but the water hadn't cooled, and the night air didn't prickle her skin as it had on the way in.

Cosette stepped out into her shoes, then said, "Oh!"

She turned back to the tub and pulled out both dripping, sopping dresses. She looked at her fairy godmère sheepishly. "I meant to put them on the wall to dry . . ."

The fairy sighed, looking between the fabric and Cosette. "Did you now?"

Cosette blushed and started wringing water back into the tub.

The fairy raised her hand. "They can do it."

At another shrill whistle, the glowbugs came back and lifted the clothes away. They wrung the dresses out, draped them along the stone wall, and dried them with a flurry of wings.

"S'il vous plaît, what are they?" Cosette asked.

The fairy looked at her sharply. "You cannot see them?"

"Non, désolé." Though she wasn't quite sure why she was apologizing.

"I . . . suppose I cannot say."

Cosette looked at her in surprise.

"I cannot talk about such things . . . here. In your realm." She looked uncomfortable with having said that much.

Cosette had so many questions, but before she could ask them, the glowbugs were back, draping the material over Cosette's head and tugging the robe away at the same time.

"Now, shall we create a different ensemble? We do not want the guests to think you have only one dress, now do we? I would not be a very good fairy godmère otherwise."

"But still in blue?" she asked hopefully.

The fairy sighed. "There are so many other colors, Mademoiselle . . . especially pink. With your coloring, perhaps a deep rose color—"

Every once in a while, so rare it always surprised her, a fierceness welled up in Cosette, a firm insistence that she have her way, that she would not be budged. She felt this now, and although there was momentary embarrassment over so little a thing, her jaw firmed and her chin lifted. "Blue."

The fairy sighed once more. "Fine. In blue."

This dress was baby blue, with stomacher and underskirt in a pure white that only the richest could afford—and afford to keep clean—and every inch of the dress shimmered like the glowbugs themselves were sewn into it.

Cosette couldn't help but regret that this dress would poof away with the sunrise.

As the fairy crafted something stunning out of nothing but her magic and some rags, Cosette bounced on the balls of her feet, more than ready to go back to that ball and attempt to speak with Gautier.

Tonight, no amount of dancing, no matter how much she loved it, would distract her from her goal.

25

PRINCESS CENDRILLON

"Cendrillon does not suit you."

Cosette glanced up sharply, almost missing a step. "Pardon, Monsieur?"

He smiled, the man in the red frock coat, his eyes warm, as he led her in yet another dance. One Cosette found herself unable to refuse.

"Cendrillon, it is not right for you. Fleur, Léa, Antoinette —never Cendrillon. Never a cinder girl."

Cosette blushed to the roots of her hair, unable to look him in the eye. His words were so pleasing, yet always on the cusp of making her uncomfortable. She still couldn't say why.

She had no problem with flattery, and flirting was a second language to her. But what she felt with this man . . . she couldn't figure it out.

"Come now, I meant no offense." He drew her hand to his lips and kissed it, spinning her out and back again. "Won't you tell me your real name? How I might find you again? Why you so desperately seek an audience with Gautier?"

His questions piled on until she was almost gasping with the need to tell someone.

"I—I'm looking for the huntress!" she blurted.

He paled. "The huntress?"

"Oui. The huntress who . . . kills wolves. For Gautier." She looked past him, eyes darting everywhere for escape, feeling as though she should not be telling him this. "I have need of her . . . services . . . and rumor has it that she was last employed by Gautier. So . . . I need to find him. To meet him. To ask him. Where I might find her."

Cosette snapped her mouth closed, humiliated that she'd told this man so much. This, this *stranger*.

What was it about him that he could wrest her secrets from her? That he could get her to agree to so many dances?

Yet she couldn't help but be flattered by his attention, the way he singled her out. The way he kept asking, not taking no for an answer.

Not that her nos were very convincing to herself, even.

Or how much she wished she could simply enjoy her time with him instead of wishing she were with Gautier instead.

He wore the same red frock coat, as if he wanted to make sure she recognized him, though now he also wore a navy blue vest and tan breeches, instead of the all-black vest and breeches of before.

Cosette spoke fervently, her voice just loud enough so he could hear her, but not so their conversation would carry.

He pulled her closer than warranted to hear.

"I've heard he was the last to hire her before she disappeared. If anyone could know where she is, how to find her, it would be he, surely."

The man she danced with looked positively flummoxed. "This Gautier . . . you still have not met him?"

She shook her head. "I'm not even sure what he looks like. I was hoping to find him. And in turn, her." She looked up at him with wide, earnest, wistful eyes. "Might you help me find him, Monsieur? S'il vous plaît? It would mean the world to me."

His eyes glittered, his expression far too pleased that she

was asking him for assistance. "But of course, Mademoiselle." He spread one hand wide, off to the side. "I am happy to say that Gautier—"

At that moment, the music ended with a flourish, the crush of people clapped, cutting off whatever he had been about to say, and Cosette was once more swarmed with gentlemen eager to dance with her.

She could've sworn he growled, "You've got to be kidding me," but she was too busy straining to see where he'd been pointing. But she could see nothing in this crowd.

Excusing herself, Cosette hurried over to where he'd gestured, but she saw no one that matched the brief glimpse she'd had of him, and no one she asked knew where Gautier had gone. Many reiterated that he disappeared every night, only to reappear for the final announcement.

Something Cosette already knew.

Something she was coming to dread.

Despair swept over her. How was she to find Gautier if he made himself scarce every evening?

She simply must find him. Tonight.

With a determined step, Cosette turned and left the ball-room, seeking another way to gain an audience with Gautier. To make him listen.

26

THE HUNTRESS IS MY SISTER

osette tried to sneak upstairs, to get to the family suites to listen at doors and beg an audience. But each staircase to the uppermost floors was well guarded, and no one would let her pass, no matter how much she pleaded or tried to bargain. Nor could she find an opportunity to slip past.

Apparently she was not the first to try such a tactic.

True, she had one more night, but she was close to despairing of ever speaking with Gautier.

How could she find him if he did not wish to be found?

She crept back down the stairs, in the east wing that led to the refreshment rooms for Mesdemoiselles, when a prickling sensation swept over her exposed skin. She rubbed her arms and looked up.

Stasie was staring right at her, eyes wide.

Cosette froze.

They stayed locked there, staring at each other, neither moving.

Then a pair of ladies walked between them, laughing, and Cosette ran down the stairs, heart pounding.

The fairy godmother said she wouldn't be recognized, but

Stasie had. She'd recognized her, even with the masque on. Even with the fairy's kiss. But how?

It didn't matter how. It only mattered that she had.

She veered for the open doors, but there stood Druce, laughing and talking with a knot of young Messieurs and Mesdemoiselles blocking the exit.

She caught their attention, or rather, her monstrous dress did. Their eyes lit, especially Druce's, and they started toward her, calling friendly greetings.

But nothing close to recognition lit this stepsister's eyes. Thank heavens.

Cosette dipped a curtsey. "Forgive me. I am . . . meeting someone."

Hiding behind her fan, pale pink this time, to match the tone of her dress, she fluttered it as if she were warm and practically ran for the ballroom.

She passed a mirror on the way and did a double take.

There, in her hair, a monstrous bright-pink flower blossomed, drowning her crown and curls and covering nearly half of her head. Cosette sighed.

Once again, her Fée Marraine had made her displeasure known at Cosette's insistence upon having another blue dress.

A small smile found its way onto her face.

Perhaps she would let her create a pink dress tomorrow evening? It was the least she could do after such kindness.

But if she could find Gautier tonight, she would have no need to come back tomorrow. In fact, she may not be *able* to come back tomorrow.

Especially if Stasie had recognized her.

The thought rushed her on, and she hurried through the throngs of dancers, as close to the fringes as she could manage, intent on getting to the gardens and escaping. But her eyes swept the room, looking for Gautier a final time.

She still hadn't met him. She still hadn't asked him about her sister.

But none of that would matter if she were murdered by her stepmère and never saw the light of day again.

So Cosette picked up her skirts and ran for the exit.

On the way, she passed the man in the red frock coat. His eyes lighted, and he held out his hand. "May I have this dance, Mademoiselle?"

She met his eyes, and his expression changed.

"Why, ma belle Mademoiselle, whatever is the matter?"

She just shook her head and kept going.

He followed her. "Mademoiselle, please wait! I don't even know your name."

But there were too many people crowding her, too many people wanting to dance with her, and fear of discovery pulsed a pounding beat in her temples.

She couldn't push through to the exit, no matter how hard she tried. So she did the only thing she could think of. She fluttered her eyelashes and began to swoon.

"Mademoiselle!" He was at her side in an instant. "Back, get back! Give her room to breathe."

She daren't smile, but she sincerely wanted to tease Rose about how effective her methods were. No matter that Rosette would roll her eyes and tell her she was being ridiculous.

Flirting was a second language to her, and it worked.

As she'd hoped, the man in the red coat caught her up, unable to carry her with the sheer amount of dress she wore, and hustled her into the garden.

Cosette leaned heavily on him.

He settled her on a bench and leaned far too close to take in her face in the candlelight spilling from within. "Are you well, dearest Mademoiselle?"

Cosette flicked her fan open and fluttered it between them, as breathless as she could make herself. "Oh, forgive me! I do not know what came over me."

Rose could say what she will, but all Cosette had to do was look down and bat her eyelashes, something she'd found to be most devastating on those of the masculine sex, and he was almost beside himself to help her.

By the smitten look on his face, it was working beautifully.

A servant brought water, and she was soon supplied with smelling salts—which she was careful to keep far away from her nose—a handkerchief, and a small plate of chocolates to make her feel better.

She dabbed her forehead and neck with the damp hand-kerchief, made the chocolates disappear, and eyed the edge of the garden, wondering how quickly she could recover and make her escape.

"About Gautier . . ."

Instantly he had her full attention. "Oui?"

"If I were to gain you an audience . . . why is it so important that you find the huntress? Could you not hire one of Gautier's many other huntsmen? I hear they are all quite good at what they do. More than good, actually. The best."

"Truly?" Cosette jumped to her feet and clasped her hands under her chin. "Could you truly get me in to see him?"

He smiled, a bit too smugly, and rose to tower over her. "It's a distinct possibility."

She chose to ignore it. "Oh, I would be ever so grateful. Might we go now? It is ever so urgent—"

She lifted her skirts and started to rush back toward the château, but the man caught her arm. "I'm afraid I can't interrupt him until I know *why* you wish to see him. Very few gain an audience, and I'm afraid I can't waste his time."

Cosette looked at him with wide eyes, stricken.

"Not that I think you would ever waste his time," he hastened to say. "Simply that I would be unable to get you in if it were not . . . something unique. Something that would capture his attention."

Cosette stared up at the château, strains of revelry drifting out into the night, and wondered if he truly could get her in to see him, or if he were making himself seem more important than he really was.

"My sister," she whispered, still staring at the château.

"I beg your pardon, I did not quite hear —"

"My sister," she said, louder. Then looked at him. "The huntress is my sister."

27

MUST FLEE

*N*ow that she thought about it, she supposed she shouldn't have sprung such information on the poor man. At least not quite so suddenly.

So she started prattling to cover her nerves, and she sincerely hoped he heard some of what she said past the dazed look in his eyes.

"You see, the last I heard from her was right before she took a job for Gautier. She always keeps in touch with me, always, but I have had nothing but silence for about a year now."

The man looked as if he were having trouble keeping up. "Your . . . sister?"

"Oui, a most beloved sister." Cosette turned her most beseeching look upon him. "It is my dearest wish to find out what happened to her, where she might be. I will pay anything! I have jewels . . ."

Her voice trailed off as she realized she hadn't kept any for herself. How could she, when her stepmère kept her locked up and demanded each one?

But she had a way to pay. And if it was the only way to see Gautier . . .

She reached down to slip off her shoes.

His jaw tightened at the mention of payment, and Cosette froze. She bit her lip, uncertain.

"Are we . . . talking about the same huntress?" the man said with a strained quality to his voice.

"But of course. None other than the mighty huntress, Ro LeFèvre, a favorite of Gautier's." She was quick to add, "If the rumors are to be believed. She would never dare say such a thing of herself."

At the stunned look on his face, Cosette whipped out a lacy handkerchief from her sleeve and dabbed her eyes, covertly looking for the best way out of the garden and a quick escape. This had not gone according to her plan in the least.

Especially since she was pouring her heart out to someone who was decidedly *not* Gautier.

"Your name . . . it is LeFèvre?" he asked.

"Oh non, Monsieur. It is not, and I beg of you to stop asking me. My family, were they to find out—it would not go well for me."

He didn't seem to know what to say to that.

"But you are . . . royalty? A princess?"

Now Cosette didn't know what to say.

She'd said it, therefore there had to be some truth in it. But was it only her disguise? The persona she took on when she fled her mundane life? The persona her Fée Marraine let her borrow for an evening? She hadn't yet been able to ask.

It was the only thing that made sense.

"Please, Monsieur, I despair of ever seeing my sister again. Can you do it? Can you get me in to see him? Gautier? This very night?"

"I'm afraid that is impossible, Mademoiselle, but—"

"Oh, I knew you would not be able to! Only I had hoped —" Cosette's eyes filled with tears, and she swiped them away, upset with herself for trusting him.

She didn't mind pretending to cry, but she most certainly didn't want to *truly* cry in front of a complete stranger, one who'd crushed all her hopes and dreams in one fell blow.

After she'd handed him the cudgel with which to do it.

He once again snatched up her hand and placed a reverent kiss upon it, making Cosette jump, the move so sudden. "Fret not, dear belle. You are right. If anyone knows where the huntress might be, surely it is Gautier. But perhaps . . . I might know a thing as well, though it is only a rumor."

At the hope in her eyes, he held up a hand, looking very grave indeed.

"Alas, rumor has it that she has been on a mission this past year, a mission so secretive, no one has heard from her in all that time, not even Gautier."

Cosette gasped and sat down hard. Thankfully he directed her to the bench just in time.

The last she'd spoken to her sister, she was off on that horrible mission for Gautier, and she'd come to say goodbye.

And Cosette hadn't heard from her since.

If she'd known that would be the last time she'd see her, if she'd known that would be her final goodbye . . .

She would've never left Rosette in that treehouse. She would've never let Rosette go off by herself. She would've followed her to the ends of the earth, would've been a part of her story, of her . . . ending.

Then her père had married that awful woman while her sisters married any man who would take them while her brothers fled the house to their apprenticeships while her father had gambled away their country estate while he'd dropped her off to live with her stepmère and awful stepsisters while he went off and spent even more money he didn't have—

All this spiraled through Cosette in seconds and threatened to choke the life out of her.

She swallowed convulsively, willing herself not to break down and sob in front of this . . . well, whoever he was.

He sat next to her, too close, and wrapped one arm around her waist, still holding her hand with the other. "Mademoiselle, what can I do to wipe the sorrow from your brow?"

She turned to him, his face less than a breath away, and met his eyes with her huge ones. "Help me find my sister. Please. I want nothing more in this world."

He smiled, a slow, sultry thing, almost a smirk, and lifted her fingertips to his lips, kissing them one by one. Then he kissed the inside of her wrist, and Cosette found herself a little breathless. And distracted.

"Why then, Mademoiselle, your wish is my command."

Then his eyes settled on her lips, and he leaned forward.

Voices interrupted them. "There she is! Mademoiselle, we simply must speak with you."

Druce's group of young adults hurried toward her, delight on their faces. Stasie trailed behind, staying as far back as she possibly could.

Cosette gasped and jumped to her feet. "Oh, is it truly so late?" She looked down at the startled man, the one who was so close to promising her an audience with Gautier—who'd nearly *kissed* her. "Forgive me."

And she took off running.

Carriage once again forgotten.

"Mademoiselle, wait! If I cannot know your name, how do I find you?"

But she did not wait. She ran straight into the garden, making for the fields and the thick forest beyond.

"Désolé!" Cosette called over one shoulder.

She had to get back before Stasie told the Comtesse, before Druce recognized her, before any of them found out she'd once more been able to attend the ball.

She just barely heard him make a frustrated noise before

he called out, "Guards! Give chase and detain that . . . running woman."

She nearly fell headlong at the shouted words. He was calling the guards? For simply running away?

Oh no, he wasn't.

Going to stop her, that was.

Cosette slipped off her shoes so she could run faster, and as she bent hastily and scooped them up, she missed one.

She paused to go back, but guards were already running after her, and her stepmère would kill her if she were caught. So Cosette used every ounce of speed she possessed and ran as she'd never run before.

Let them try to catch her.

28

LET OUT FOR WATER

Cosette jolted awake as her stepmère's closet flooded with light. She didn't even remember how she got in, but she did know she was tired, sore, and most definitely had not had enough sleep.

As soon as her eyes adjusted, Stasie's outline came into view. Cosette brightened a mere second before dread dropped low in her belly. Stasie had seen her. She *knew* Cosette had sneaked out. She held her breath and waited for Stasie to speak.

Stasie nervously cleared her throat. "Maman says you can come out now. To make our breakfast."

Cosette's eyebrow climbed her forehead. No apology? No remorse? Just "come cook for us"?

She almost didn't get up. The long nights were wearing on her, the prospect of being chained to the table too much to bear.

But tonight was the last night of the ball. If she didn't get up, if she didn't cook and clean and do everything like normal, her stepmère might suspect, and she might do more to keep her here. She couldn't risk that.

Besides, it was better than being locked up. Wasn't it?

Slowly, oh so slowly, in more pain than she cared to admit, Cosette got to her feet and left the pitch-black room where her stepmère kept her valuables locked away.

Where she kept Cosette locked away.

She was almost to the bedroom door when Stasie called out, "I know!"

Cosette froze, not daring to move another step.

"What you did. Sneaking out."

Slowly, ever so carefully, Cosette faced her stepsister.

Her face must have been fierce, because Stasie blanched and took a hasty step back.

"But I didn't tell anyone. Not yet."

"Nor will you," Cosette all but growled.

Surprisingly, jewels still fell from her lips. It wasn't kind, and it wasn't like her, but the jewels apparently didn't know any better.

Hunger gnawed at her, and the injustice of her imprisonment—and being expected to immediately get back to work, no apology in sight—bothered her more than if she'd been well-fed and well-rested.

Then she could ignore her mistreatment and focus on survival. On serving, on remaining in her place. On being the good, obedient little stepdaughter.

As she'd been able to do so far.

Cosette moved close as Stasie flinched back and slammed the handful of pearls into her stepsister's hands so at least *that* wouldn't be one more thing she'd tattle on.

"Stasie, I have tried and tried and tried to be nice to you, to be a sister to you, even if you won't grow your own courage and be one to me, but I swear to Dieu, if you say one word to Madame Béatrice, Drucelle, or anyone else for that matter, you *won't* like what happens."

She left it at that.

She wasn't any good with threats, and she wouldn't actually know what to do, if anything, if Stasie did tell.

So she turned and marched away, leaving the jewels scattered on the floor. She hastily pulled the little pouch from her apron pocket and tied it around her neck.

A little voice niggled in her mind that she was being just as threatening as Druce, as her stepmère. That she didn't want to be anything like them, not in word or in deed.

But first water, then rest, then perhaps remorse.

She carefully moved into the kitchen and past her stepmère, who was watching her in suspicion, chain in hand.

The first thing Cosette did was go for water—but of course there wasn't any, because she hadn't gotten it.

She turned to her stepmère without thinking. "But where is the water? From the party?"

Her stepmère's jaw went tight. "Not that I need to tell *you*, but we did not think to ask for any last night, and the four small barrels—did not last as long as I thought they might."

Cosette tried not to gloat, she really did, but some of it must have come through.

Her stepmère's eyes flashed, and she gritted out, "Hold still."

Cosette tried not to react as the heavy chain was fastened around her ankle, much harder than necessary.

Could not Rose burst through the doorway this very second and rescue her?

She blinked back tears as the hope that used to swell in her chest at such thoughts didn't come.

"Once you put away the food we were able to glean from Gautier's fête and make our breakfast, then you will take the girls to the well for our water." She looked affronted. "I do not appreciate being made to wait for our morning cleansing."

Cosette kept her head down, clenched her fists. If they hadn't kept her locked up till well past noon, she would've had everything done and waiting for them like normal.

Something she wanted to calmly explain, but found she

could not. She was almost certain if she opened her mouth, she'd start screaming and never stop.

Her Fée Marraine let her out each evening; did she not see what was happening? What they were doing to her?

What was the use of a fairy godmère if she was not able to release Cosette from this torment?

"Well? Quickly now! We haven't got all day."

She forced herself to speak. "S'il vous plaît, Stepmère, I must draw the water first. In order to make the meals."

The Comtesse's look was cold. "Then you will take Drucelle and Anastasie with you *now*. Should you fail to return, they will bear the brunt of your punishment."

Cosette quaked under that threat, as Madame Béatrice had meant for her to do, and strained away from her as she reluctantly unfastened the chain.

Her stepmère stormed out in a swirl of skirts, and Cosette fell upon her task, anything to keep the thoughts at bay, to make it through the rest of the afternoon until the carriage whisked her away. Whisked them all away.

Cosette used the empty barrels, brooms, and leather strips to make water yokes for her stepsisters as well, not that she had any hope that much would make it home. If they deigned to carry them at all.

Her stepsisters hurried into the room, flustered and wide eyed. Cosette handed them the water buckets wordlessly.

Druce started to object, but Cosette barked at her to take it. Eyes wide, Druce did as she said, which surprised them both.

Cosette immediately set out. Weak as she was, hungry as she was, she needed water to make all the meals expected of her.

And she needed to feel the woods under her feet more than anything.

Stasie and Druce followed behind, not bothering to talk to her the whole way.

29

WORK BOOTS

osette had almost despaired of going to the ball by the time she found herself in the garden.

Her Fée Marraine was breathless. "Have you the dress? The shoes?"

Cosette ran inside and was back in moments, pulling the dress over her head.

The fairy godmother peered down at Cosette's work boots. She did not look pleased. "Whatever happened to the glass slippers?"

Cosette blushed. "I'm afraid I—lost one."

"Lost one." Now the fey woman looked even less pleased.

"Je suis désolé." Cosette reluctantly pulled out the single shoe from the set of pockets she had tied on under her dress of swirling rags and showed her.

The fairy eyed the shoe, then Cosette, then grumbled a little. "I'm afraid I do not have another pair. Make sure you don't kick your heels up too highly tonight."

"I understand." Cosette returned the shoe to its hiding spot.

"Now shoo. Off with you! It's your last night, but you'll still want to be back well before dawn."

"Oui, Madame," Cosette said meekly, still feeling contrite. She hated to ask, but . . . "The jewels?"

If she didn't know better, Cosette could've sworn the fairy gave her an annoyed look. Fairies couldn't get annoyed, could they? "The magic was tied to the shoes. Without them . . . I don't know. Wear a veil?"

"But the dress . . ."

"Was transformed, not fey made." She sighed, deeply. "I suppose I could reverse my gift, though I would rather not. Have you saved enough?" she asked severely.

Cosette could only shake her head, not explain. The wound of not being believed—by either woman—ran deep. "Non, je suis désolé."

"Being sorry won't matter a vineyard of grapes if you have nothing for the future. Have you any sense in your head at all?"

Cosette's face burned. She minded being belittled by her stepfamily, of course she did, but it was even worse coming from her Fée Marraine. "Please, godmère, I had no choice—"

"Yes, yes, a ball simply couldn't come through without spending all your wealth. How could I not understand?"

Now a little anger flushed through Cosette. "Food, firewood, clothes that aren't threadbare—oui, I see how that would be frivolous."

The woman gave her a sharp look. "Sass does not become you. I have seen the dresses and lace and feathers and combs and more your stepfamily wear, a new dress every night for these past seven evenings—"

"And yet I wear only what you share with me."

"I am merely saying that you need to *save* some of what I have given you . . ."

"And I am saying that I had no choice!"

Cosette's sharp words echoed away into the trees. They stared at each other, eyes wide, Cosette's chest heaving, the moment pregnant with tension, strain, and potential strife.

Who knew what the fey creature would do to her for her outburst? But Cosette couldn't make herself regret it.

Then the fairy godmère sighed and rubbed a hand down her face. "Forgive me, ma chère. I am under a great deal of strain in my own kingdom. I should not have taken it out on you."

Cosette snapped back the argument that had begun to form and instead stared at her Fée Marraine with her mouth parted.

The fact that the fairy was too busy with her own affairs to watch over Cosette every moment hadn't even occurred to her.

The older woman took her hands into her own and spoke gently. "I do care for you, and I know I can be . . . harsher . . . than I mean to be, but I also worry for you. I cannot be here as much as I would like, cannot watch over you as I should, but please, ma chère, I beg of you, take my words to heart. The curse is nowhere near being broken, and I fear you have many hard days ahead of you. Please, find a way to save *some* of my gift for those hard times."

She cupped Cosette's cheek in her hand and gave her such a kind, motherly look, Cosette's eyes filled with tears. The fairy kissed her forehead, then moved away and turned brusque and businesslike once more.

"If you want to keep from spilling gems all over the young Messieurs you dance with, keep your shoe in your pocket. It is not a perfect solution, and you may yet want to wear a veil and that pouch around your neck, but it should help. At least a little."

Cosette nodded and swallowed, still taking in everything she'd said. How did she know about the curse? How long it might last?

And who might be trying to break it?

"I think midnight blue tonight, with diamonds that glitter like the stars. What do you think of a high collar in the back and a swooping V at the front? I saw something like it recently in my travels . . ."

As the fairy detailed her designs, Cosette relaxed and gave herself over to the transformation.

She'd try to figure out how to hide a few of the gems in a way she could still honestly say she hadn't.

Her stepmère didn't believe her, after all.

Why not prove her right?

30

PLEASE STAY

In the end, she decided against the veil. If every once in a while a pearl rolled onto the floor or a flower petal fell, it was hardly noticed in the bustle and soon crushed underfoot or plucked up by some enterprising, eagle-eyed person who had relieved their hosts of several such nothings and had no problem snatching up a few more.

But she hid behind her fan every time she spoke, just in case, and spoke as little as possible.

Her smiles were more effective anyway.

Cosette's new dress drew even more attention than the other two. Tonight, she'd quickly discovered her boots—which were still boots, but transformed—her fan, and a band of rosettes at the base of her crown were all a deep rose pink, but tasteful and perfectly accenting the midnight blue of her gown.

And they all glittered as much as her dress.

She had to admit the fairy had outdone herself, but she found it hard to enjoy any of it.

This was her last night to approach Gautier. To find out if he knew of her sister's whereabouts.

Surely she wasn't actually . . . missing.

She refused to believe it.

Cosette tried to smile, tried to laugh at the attention, to enjoy the swarms wanting to dance with her, but it was strained at best.

But of course no one noticed. They were all too enamored of being close to her, of seeking fame through hers, of perhaps unmasking the mystery of who she was.

A familiar voice broke through the revelry. "Might I have this dance?"

Cosette turned, knowing whom she would find, red frock coat never absent.

If it were military, she would understand, but she could think of no other reason he wore it nightly than for her to be able to find him, as they were all masked.

It wasn't as if she could hide.

She hoped she could say she would recognize him anywhere, but she could not have said the same for any other young Monsieur with whom she danced.

Perhaps she was grateful for the red frock coat.

That is, once she saw to a little matter first.

"Not going to send your guards after me if I refuse, are you?" She smiled sweetly at him.

He winced. "That was, perhaps, not my best moment."

"Surely not."

"Might you honor me with a dance anyway? Give me a chance to make it up to you?"

She nodded, more so not to be rude with so many eyes watching than any true desire to dance with him. He swept her close.

Well, as close as he could, with her fairy godmère's latest creation. Which had the most impressive amount of lace and layers yet.

At least she'd convinced the fairy not to subject her to the awful pouf of towering hair that had just come into fashion when the curse fell.

And at least her Fée Marraine hadn't turned her hair pink out of spite.

Which had also been in fashion before the curse fell. That and lemon yellow and powdered blue and leaf green and storm gray.

Speaking of pink, she'd been so flustered in the garden, she'd completely forgotten to ask for a pink dress. Perhaps she could make it up to her fairy godmère another way?

Cosette startled as the Monsieur spoke close to her ear.

"I deeply apologize, Mademoiselle, for my careless actions in the garden. Would you do me the honor of forgiving me?"

It took her a moment to pull herself back into the conversation. "On one condition."

"Name it."

"Tell me why you did it?" She tilted her head while she awaited his response. She couldn't help teasing him, just a little. "Then I'll consider it."

He cleared his throat and adjusted his cravat. "A moment of insanity."

At her wide-eyed look, he smiled.

"I panicked. I didn't know how to find you, and I feared you would not return, especially after not gaining an audience with, ahem, Gautier. A fear that has scarcely been relieved with how late you were."

Cosette flushed at the question in his eyes. "I was . . . detained. But I had every intention of attending this evening, I assure you. As you can see."

"Bon." He positively beamed at her. "You see, I have something of import to tell you."

He waited to continue until he held her rapt attention, which was hardly any wait at all. He pulled her close and whispered next to her ear, so that others nearby might not hear, it seemed.

There was simply no other reason for him to do so, and no logical reason for Cosette's heart to flutter so.

"Gautier has promised a most tantalizing announcement this evening. I cannot help but hope that some of your questions might be answered. If you stay for the very end, that is."

Hope swelled in her chest, fierce and hot, but was instantly doused by her fairy godmère's warnings.

"I dare not stay so late, Monsieur."

He pulled back to look at her. "Why ever not?"

"I . . . could not say."

His confusion turned to smugness. "Then I simply will not take your refusal for the answer of your heart. You wish to stay, do you not?"

Cosette nodded, too overcome to hide how desperately she wished to do so.

"Then you shall. And I shall help you."

A small smile curved Cosette's lips. "And how do you plan to do that, Monsieur?"

"Why"—he spun her out and back again—"by staying close to your side the entire evening, but of course."

Cosette started to object, but he cut her off.

"And do not try to tell me society will judge us. I simply do not care."

This time, her smile was as wide as his own. "Then how could I possibly refuse?"

His smile turned kind, tender, and stirred up all kinds of things Cosette had been longing to feel in someone's arms. "There's the answer I was looking for."

31

LAST NIGHT OF THE BALL

Despair seemed to descend in a thick cloud the later the evening became. It didn't matter what Gautier would say to the crowds—she had to get back before the sun rose.

Her fairy godmère said her life depended upon it.

Surely those were not empty words, oui?

She thought over the past three nights, each playing itself out in her mind as she danced.

Every night the man in the red coat sought her out. Every night he danced with her.

Cosette couldn't help but be flattered by the attention, but she also couldn't help being frustrated that she hadn't yet spoken to Gautier, hadn't yet been able to find anything out about her sister.

Yet every night, he listened patiently, with understanding in his touch and gaze, and every night, Cosette poured out just a little more of her story. Could she trust him, really?

And every night, he asked who she was, begged her to allow him to call on her, requested that she not leave so early or so hastily.

And every night, she slipped from his grasp and hurtled

home, desperate to arrive before Gautier finished his speech, to be back in her stepmère's closet, pretending to sleep, before her absence was discovered and the sun ended a night of revelry.

But this night, the last night of the ball, she couldn't pretend to be elated by the beauty, food, and laughter that surrounded her.

If this night passed as every other, Gautier would be lost to her, and through him, her sister.

No matter what this Monsieur might say.

As she danced with the man in the masque, red coat with brass buttons never absent, he caught her up close to him, closer than the dance warranted.

"What saddens you, Mademoiselle? On so glorious a night?"

A tear dripped onto her cheek.

"Ah, ma belle Mademoiselle, say it isn't so! A tear? Now I must know what ails you. Are you in pain, perhaps? Or is it a pain of the heart? Surely not one of these devils"—one hand swept wide to encompass the rest of the room—"has captured your heart as I have!"

Cosette spoke quickly, more to break off his flamboyant gesturing and increasingly ridiculous phrasing—which had not improved as the night wore on. "It is not you, Monsieur, truly. I have yet to see or even speak to Monsieur DuBois. You know I cannot get close to him without help. And I simply must speak with him!"

She choked on a sob, biting her lip to keep it from escaping.

"Because of your sister?" he asked carefully.

"Oui," she whispered, unable to keep her heartbreak from escaping in the broken sound.

"Tell me more about her. Please."

So she did. She told them of their childhood. Of her brothers and sisters. How she and Rose had been the closest, always there for each other, even when the others were jealous or treated them like they were too young or stupid to join them in anything.

Her mouth ran away with her—it felt so good to talk to someone who genuinely wanted to hear her troubles—and more spilled out than she meant to tell.

She wasn't sure when it happened. But at some point, light crept into his eyes, he fought a smile, and Cosette knew she was found out.

She gasped. "Oh, please, Monsieur, tell no one! I—I am not supposed to be here. If my family . . ."

"Your stepfamily, you mean."

Her heart dropped right past her toes.

Her mind filed back through what she'd said, but she couldn't figure out what had revealed her identity.

Rose had used their mère's maiden name, LeFèvre, to distance her family from her reputation, to keep them safe. And Cosette had just let this *stranger* know her closely guarded secret.

"Please, I am begging you."

He raised her hands to his lips. "You have nothing to fear from me, Mademoiselle."

"Not even Gautier. Promise me."

His eyes twinkled. "Not even Gautier."

He seemed to be laughing at her, but Cosette couldn't for the life of her figure out why.

As the song was winding down, he said, "I shall get us drinks, non?"

"Oui, s'il vous plaît."

She would use the time he was distracted and fighting the crowds to escape.

The final song of the evening ended, he gave her a sweeping bow, then was lost to the crowd. Cosette turned to make her way home, her fairy godmother's warning echoing in her head.

But before she could, the crowd pressed forward, eager to hear what Gautier might say.

Cosette's steps slowed. It was the final night of the ball. What could it hurt to hear Gautier's speech?

Even if she stayed past when the sun rose, even if her dress dissolved into rags around her, at least Gautier would notice her.

She would *make* him notice her.

She paused, head tilted, ideas barreling through her at the speed of racing horses.

Even if her stepfamily called her out, berated her, she would raise her voice, call out to him, and he would see her. Hear her. Whether her disguise held or not.

Cosette had to wait for the perfect opportunity to make herself heard.

It wasn't long until he came out to much cheering, and Cosette stared up at him in awe.

Strong, tall, handsome—she could instantly see why the crowd was enamored with him. She was halfway enamored herself.

Gautier began a grand speech, which filled the room to bursting with his presence.

He spoke of how he'd fallen in love with their town, with their people. How he hoped to come back.

His voice was deep and carried to the edges of the room. He wore a fine green frock coat with gold buttons, and his waistcoat and breeches were made from cloth-of-gold, cloth woven from pure gold.

He struck a fine figure, and Cosette may have fluttered her fan just a little harder.

Also, from the balustrade, he appeared to be quite broad shouldered. It was hard to tell, with the Montagnes standing along the wall behind him, but he seemed to tower over them.

But she couldn't make out much else from her distance,

and he didn't seem like anyone she'd met. Though a few of his mannerisms were familiar . . .

She simply needed to get closer.

Cosette tried to edge forward, but it was just so crowded. No one budged or stepped out of her way, not even with a polite, "Excusez-moi, s'il vous plaît."

But his next words stopped her cold.

"Many of you have heard rumors that I have been looking for a bride to continue my legacy, to ensure the DuBois line is able to safeguard France for generations to come. Well I am happy to report that these are not simply rumors."

Light laughter sprinkled throughout the throng, but giddy squeals came from one particular direction.

She strained up on her tiptoes to see past the crowd, but she was too short. So she tried to see between bodies instead.

The crowd shifted just enough, and there were Druce and Stasie and her stepmère, beaming up at Gautier as he beamed back at them.

Oh no. It couldn't be. Surely not! Gautier would never align himself with her stepfamily, would he?

But of course he would. They were perfectly amiable in public, and either of her stepsisters would look stunning on his arm.

And suddenly her plans of calling out to him seemed futile, of ever being the recipient of his aid nothing but a dream.

He would never help her. Not if Drucelle or Anastasie had caught his eye.

And suddenly the danger seemed that much more real. Of her being caught. Of whatever her Fée Marraine had warned her of.

Cosette knew she should move, knew she should get back to the closet well before her stepmère, knew she shouldn't risk staying.

But her feet couldn't move. She *had* to hear what he was

going to say next. To make sure he wasn't going to say what she thought he was.

"I am pleased to announce that I have found the perfect person, my better half, the most beautiful Mademoiselle in all the realm! Someone who makes me most happy to relinquish my bachelorhood. Though I didn't know such a thing was possible myself."

More laughter.

Gautier sobered, his deep voice carrying to the far reaches of the room. "I *have* chosen a bride, though I didn't know that was my intention, and I am happy that what I thought was a far-distant occasion is upon us. Me, specifically."

He could've said anything, he was so well-loved, and the people would've humored him with cheers or laughter, but this was over the top.

Cosette fidgeted, wanting the people to quiet, wanting Gautier to *get on* with his point. To make sure he wasn't saying what she thought he might be.

That he had chosen Stasie or Drucelle.

She needed to go. Her Fée Marraine had warned her. She was in danger.

Yet her feet remained rooted where they were.

"And as my gift to you, not only has a full wagon train from the Mesdemoiselles of the Mountain arrived, your town has been added to the permanent rotation. You will no longer have to go seeking it, nor fear missing it for months on end!"

The crowd cheered until the chandeliers shook and Cosette could've sworn she felt a rumble in the marble under her feet.

Joy leapt in her heart for this one small victory, followed swiftly by fear of discovery, and the general tumult finally freed her to move toward the exit.

"But who is she?" someone called once they could be heard.

Cosette froze. Peeked over her shoulder.

Gautier spread his hands wide. "I daren't announce it till I speak to the young Mademoiselle's family, non?"

The crowd grumbled, and Gautier laughed, sounding delighted to have the crowd so firmly in his enthrall.

"Never fear, you shall be the first to hear of it once the happy lady says yes. Until then, take as much food as you can carry! The wagons are full to bursting."

Cosette turned and pushed her way through the crowd, desperate to reach the doorway before it became unsurpassable.

The last thing he called before chaos descended was: "There is enough food for everyone!"

He tried to say more, then gave up with a laugh as cheering and shouting made his words unintelligible.

She had no need to get his attention tonight; if her stepfamily's reactions were anything to go by, he would be at her very doorstep on the morrow.

To propose to one of her awful stepsisters.

32

MUST OUTRUN THE SUN

No matter how fast she tried to run, her steps kept slowing without her permission.

Running in work boots didn't help.

Nor did the fact that she couldn't find the carriage the one time she'd actually remembered to look for it.

She was exhausted. From barely sleeping. From dancing all night, then running home, through the woods, before the sun came up.

For the past three nights.

She stumbled, almost fell, and hauled herself upright.

The sky was becoming an alarming shade of blue.

Sure, she'd cut it close a few times, but she was always in the house before the sun rose, hiding her clothing and shoes, then back in the closet, somehow, before the sky brightened fully.

She would not make it this morning. That much was abundantly clear.

And she could barely fight with her dress past all the brambles and branches.

Normally she slipped through them as if they were not

really there: she, a sprite flitting through, unable to be touched; the branches, bending to her will.

Now she ran as if pushing through the waves of the sea while the waves pushed her steadily back to shore.

She was steps from the boundary line to her stepfamily's estate when the sun peeked over the horizon.

Flames erupted all around her, and she screamed.

Searing heat flashed from the top of her dress all the way down, the sun's rays burning her dress, scorching her skin with the intense heat.

She fought to get the dress off, but it was massive, and it was too hot, and it was burning.

She cried and fought and tried to pull it from her, but she couldn't. The heat was unbearable.

Within seconds, it turned to embers, the flames winking out, the fabric wisping away from her in glowing specks, until the fey magic burned away into nothing.

She stood there, in the forest, in her underclothes, holding herself and shivering from the fear, from the cold, from her pounding heart.

Shaking, she stared down at her arms, certain they would be blistered and oozing, but they were only a light red, as if she'd stood too close to the fireplace. It faded, even as she watched.

Her underclothes were scorched and smoking, though.

She slumped against a tree, no longer able to remain upright, and took deep breaths to calm her racing heart.

Her Fée Marraine couldn't have warned her that her *dress would catch on fire* if touched by sunlight?

Thank the Creator she hadn't burned with it.

"Your life depends upon it." Cosette blinked as the words echoed in her head.

Gasping, she tore into the set of pockets she'd tied on under her dress and came out with her glass slipper. It remained intact, though it looked as if it had been shattered, cracks spiderwebbing in every direction.

Had the shoe saved her life? Since she carried it with her?

With a cry, he held it close to her heart, bending her head and whispering, "Merci, Fée Marraine, merci beaucoup."

Jewels fell to the forest floor, and she stared at them.

She needed to hide them. And her throat raged with thirst.

Falling to her knees, she dug them out of the decaying and blackened leaves. She cradled them gently in her shoe, carefully returned it to the pocket with the least holes, then stumbled to her feet and ran for the well.

33

BACK IN THE CLOSET

Hardly able to haul up the water with her shaking arms, Cosette almost cried in relief when the bucket breached the top of the well.

She guzzled from the dipper before returning the bucket to the well, then lay back in the dead grass next to it, sincerely hoping no peckish wolves would happen to wander by in the hopes of a light snack.

But even that thought didn't drive her to her feet.

She would rest, then she would return. But only for a chance to meet with Gautier. After that . . .

Eyes closed, she lay there for who knew how long until a bird's song roused her.

"Hurry, hurry! They are back! You haven't much time," it seemed to say.

She forced herself up, muscles aching, and hobbled toward the house.

Sure enough, they were back, but they were avoided easily enough as Cosette sneaked in the back way and up through the servant's staircase.

She stopped in her old room, peeled off her burned clothing, and hurried into the only other set of clothing she owned.

Both dresses were a faded gray, scratchy, homespun, made for servants, and came with an apron, so hopefully her step-family wouldn't notice she was in the other set.

Not that they ever looked closely enough at her to notice such things.

She waded the burned underclothes and shoved them under a loose floorboard, vowing to come back and finish the job of burning them later.

She only had the one set of pockets, so she tied those back on quickly, under her skirts.

Maybe she could trade more lace to the seamstress for another set of underclothes? Without her stepfamily knowing?

But she was taking too long, and her tired brain kept thinking of things that were not important right now.

She hurried downstairs, only remembering once she stood outside her stepmère's door that she was supposed to be locked inside.

The front door slammed closed, most likely after the last of their pillage had been brought inside by the servants dropping them off after the fête, and loud footsteps and shrill voices sounded in the hall.

"Fairy godmère, are you there?" Cosette whispered.

Demands were made to let Cosette out right away to bring drinks and snacks and help them change out of their clothes, but their stepmère's calm voice came next, saying they could do such things themselves.

"I'm supposed to be inside, remember?" Cosette hissed. "Fairy godmère? Can you hear me?"

Footsteps sounded on the stairs, more stomping than anything, as the three women loudly complained about the girl at the ball who had stolen everyone's attention for the entire evening. Until Gautier's announcement, of course.

Cosette paused to listen, fascinated in spite of herself.

No one knew who she was, and all the eligible young

Mademoiselles and their mères hated her and would see her burn, many had vowed. Cosette rolled her eyes.

They should have seen her in the forest, then. She nearly had.

She fingered the shoe in her pocket, remembering belatedly that she hadn't hidden the jewels. She quickly dug them out and added them to the pouch, in case her stepmère asked, then hastily tied it around her neck.

"But at least Gautier knows real women of quality!" Druce crowed. "Please, Maman, she has slept this whole time, and we must get ready for Gautier's visit. Can she not help us? This once?"

"Drucelle, how many times must I tell you—"

Cosette gasped as they reached the top of the stairs. They need merely turn their heads and see her standing there. "Fairy godmère!"

At a small noise of alarm, her head whipped to Stasie. She stared at Cosette, mouth open, as Druce and Madame Béatrice turned to Stasie.

She quickly dropped her eyes so they wouldn't look at Cosette.

"Child, whatever is the matter? You look like you've seen a phantom. You see? This is exactly why you both need to sleep before we receive Monsieur DuBois. Wake the girl *after* you've had your beauty rest. The food will keep."

Cosette felt the whisper of magic on herself and looked down.

Her dress, the beautiful midnight-blue one she'd last worn to the ball, swirled around her as if the loveliest ghost of a dress, not there but somehow visible.

She glanced up quickly, panic clanging in her head, and their eyes met again.

Her stepmère and stepsister started to turn toward her, Stasie's eyes dropped to take in the gown, and then Cosette was in the closet.

Panic fluttered in her chest. What had just happened? Did her Fée Marraine *want* her to be punished?

It seemed another cruel trick.

Cosette eased herself down, her muscles aching, too tired to stay awake and worry.

She'd find out if she was to be punished soon enough.

34

CAUGHT

When Stasie let her out, hours later, she seemed awfully chatty. Prattling on and on. Not meeting her eyes. As if trying to avoid certain topics.

By saying anything and everything of no consequence.

Cosette was grateful. She didn't know how to explain what had happened. Or if she'd dreamed it.

Entirely possible with how hard she'd slept just now.

"Maman was able to get a load of vegetables from the Mesdemoiselles' wagon master," Stasie said. "Apparently they were here for the fête, providing food because Gautier hired them."

Although she knew this, had been there for the announcement herself, Cosette's mouth flooded with saliva, and she had to swallow to keep from drooling all over herself.

It had been hours since the ball, after all, and the last thing she'd had was those chocolates.

And although the rich food from the ball had been wonderful, she couldn't wait to prepare the loveliest meals from all the fresh vegetables that never went bad.

"Bon," she said simply, and tried to move on.

She had to somehow get through this day, knowing

Gautier would be here this evening, not knowing how she would speak to him in her rags, without the barrier of her gowns and rich trappings to make him think she was someone important. Someone worth listening to.

Surely he would never listen to a servant.

"He's coming here for you, isn't he," Stasie said flatly.

Cosette jerked to a halt. And peeked over her shoulder. "Who?"

"Gautier. He's coming here. For you."

When Cosette didn't respond, Stase went on.

"I saw you at the ball, remember? And the . . . dress. In the hall. It was the same one the princess wore last night, though no matter how hard I studied you, I didn't recognize you this time. Is he coming to take you away?"

Cosette honestly couldn't get her brain to work. Why on earth did Stasie think that?

"I never even got to dance with him," Cosette tried to explain.

"Didn't dance with him?" Her stepsister was scowling, though she looked more confused than angry.

At a noise in the hallway, both girls spun toward the door.

But it didn't open.

Cosette started to move away, but Stasie grabbed her wrist and held on tight.

"Take me with you. If he comes for you, s'il vous plaît, take me. Druce too. She doesn't mean to be cruel, but it's her armor, you know? It's how she protects herself. Please, I am begging you—"

Cosette jerked her arm away, more roughly than she'd intended. "I don't even know what you're talking about! Why would Gautier come here for me? I didn't even—"

Druce shouted from the bottom of the stairs. "What's taking so long up there? Did you get lost, Stase?"

Neither girl answered.

"Don't make me come up there!"

Both girls hastened toward the door.

"Coming!" Stasie called, her voice too high pitched.

Cosette's mind was spinning. But she was too tired to figure out what it all might mean.

But she knew she was missing *something* here.

Less than two hours of sleep per night for half a week was more detrimental to her intelligence than she'd imagined.

"Just, please, think about what I said. And . . ." Stasie wrinkled her nose. "What's that smell? Did you burn something?"

Cosette froze. She'd sneaked in and changed after the ball, but she hadn't wanted to risk taking the time to cleanse herself.

Was the smell truly that noticeable?

She met Stasie's wide eyes.

"You didn't try to . . . burn anything in Maman's closet, did you?"

A laugh bubbled out of Cosette's chest and burst from her lips. She clamped a hand over her mouth and managed a "Non, of course not" through her fingers.

Stasie looked back at the closet, as if afraid to check, so Cosette hurried downstairs, right past Druce.

Druce crossed her arms and scowled. "There's quite a mess in the kitchen, peasant. Enjoyed sleeping in, did you?"

Cosette hurried past without engaging, and surprisingly, Druce let her go.

Take me with you. Druce too.

Not what she'd expected from Stasie. But if she was asking for help, seeking a way out . . . Cosette couldn't in good conscience refuse her.

One thing was clear: Stase wanted out as much as she did. And if Stase said Druce did too, well then, she'd just have to believe her. Because all evidence said otherwise.

Cosette scanned the disaster of a kitchen, her mind spinning.

Would her fairy godmère, perhaps if she asked nicely, give her one more chance? Let her have one more dress, for Gautier?

Surely he would listen to her then.

But why Stase thought Gautier was coming to see *her* . . .

She'd have to think about that. While she was cleaning up.

35

WHEN PLANS GO AWRY

osette was deep to her elbows in flour when the hair on the back of her neck rose. She was being watched. By someone overflowing with . . . hate.

She spun around, spraying precious drops of flour around her in an arc, and sure enough, her stepmère stood in the doorway, watching her with an expression that, quite honestly, scared her.

"Where did you hide the jewels?" she all but spat.

Cosette froze like a doe, her mouth open in shock. "The . . . jewels?"

"Yes, yes, the ones you hid from us while you were locked up. I've searched everywhere. Where are they?"

Cosette could only shake her head, beginning to tremble.

"You mean to tell me you were in my closet for three nights and didn't speak once?"

Cosette's mind scrambled. "I—non. I had no one to talk to." *While I was in the closet*, she added silently.

Madame Béatrice greedily eyed the jewels that fell into the wide-open pouch about Cosette's neck. She hated it, but it was just easier that way.

"Oh! But when Stasie let me out, I gave them to her. The jewels. That came out while we were talking."

Madame Béatrice's jaw tightened. "Yes, yes, she gave me those, but those were the ones she saw fall from your mouth. Where are the others?"

Cosette didn't know what to do. How to answer. Punishment lay each way she chose, and she was more scared of her stepmère than she cared to admit.

What had started as little slights and derogatory comments covered with a laugh and a smile, passed off as a witticism, had now devolved into such hatred, at times Cosette wondered if she should fear for her life.

Such as right now.

"I am waiting."

"S'il vous plaît, Madame, I beg of you. There are no others. I gave them all—"

A thought struck her, and Cosette froze in horror. At the ball, pearls and a few jewels had scattered under the dancers' feet. Very few.

But if she admitted to that, she would admit to escaping, and if Stasie hadn't actually told on her (which was a miracle all in itself), then they both would receive even more punishment.

But if Stasie *had* told and everything she'd said earlier was a lie and Madame Béatrice was simply waiting to catch Cosette in a trap . . .

Cosette raised a hand to her head, smearing flour there, feeling faint and lightheaded.

"Ah-ha! There it is. I see it in your eyes. You are hiding something, aren't you?" Madame Béatrice jumped forward and grasped Cosette's arm, shaking her with every word. "Tell me what it is, you worm. Tell me what you've done with them!"

"Non, please, I beg of you! Nothing, nothing! I hid nothing!" She squeezed her eyes shut and cringed away.

Cosette was sobbing by now, frozen in her fear, terrified to move, to act, to say the wrong thing.

Why couldn't she be more like Rosette? Her dear sister would have punched this woman, thrown Cosette over her shoulder, and ridden far away on that beast of a horse of hers to care for Cosette every day for the rest of her life.

So why couldn't Cosette do that for herself?

"You are lying. I see it in your eyes."

Cosette choked on a laugh that was more of a thinly veiled sob. It didn't matter what Cosette said. It never did.

Her stepmère released her, and Cosette dropped to the floor, covered her head with her arms, and sobbed. How could anyone be so cruel?

How could she make it stop?

"There's only one thing to be done, then," her stepmère said with great pleasure.

Cosette tried to make herself small.

Madame Béatrice wrenched her arms away from her head, and Cosette turned her face away and squeezed her eyes even tighter, waiting for the blow.

Instead, something wrapped around her head, tight, and clicked into place.

Cosette tried to gasp—her jaw wouldn't move—and turned wide, frightened eyes on her stepmère, who looked at her in triumph.

She held up an ornate key, dropped it in her pocket, and patted it twice.

"If I can't trust you *not* to lie to me, well then. You simply won't be permitted to speak outside of my presence."

She started to turn away, but then her eyes landed on the pouch around Cosette's neck. Madame Béatrice snapped the cord, leaving a line of pain around the delicate skin there.

With a cruel smile, her stepmère spun away and swished out of the room, her skirts' rustling the only sound in the sudden silence.

Cosette sat there, frozen, tears forgotten, as she slowly raised one hand to touch her face.

Leather straps. Metal lattice. A cage. To fit her face.

As if . . . as if . . . it had been *made* for her.

A noise had her spinning around, eyes wide and horrified, terror trying to wrap her mind in blind panic.

Stase and Drucelle stared back. After a moment, Drucelle burst into laughter.

"Oh, isn't this just fitting? Our fake sister, the muzzled dog!"

She bent over her knees, laughing so hard she gasped for breath.

But Stase couldn't take her eyes off Cosette, her lips tight, her face pale, a line of sweat dotting her forehead.

Had her stepmère threatened her with the same thing? Surely not.

As Druce's laughs echoed in the room, Cosette heaved herself to her feet and tried to run, but the chain around her ankle brought her up short.

She sucked in a sharp breath through her nose, banging her elbow, knee, and ankle hard on the flagstone as she fell. Her ankle wrenched painfully against the manacle.

Druce's laughter redoubled, but a sniffle came from Stasie.

Cosette curled up in a ball and covered her head with her arms until her stepsisters gave up tormenting her and left.

She could never show her face to Gautier now.

36

SPIDERS, SLUGS, AND SERPENTS

*S*he didn't know how long she lay there, in that position, until soft footsteps roused her from her grief. She curled up tighter.

But something was slipped into her apron's pocket, and the footsteps hurried away.

After she was certain she was alone, her fingers crept into her pocket.

A key.

She sat up. Pulled it out, inspected it. It wasn't the bright gold one her stepmère had just shown her, the one to the monstrosity on her face, but the pewter one that went to her chains.

Tears rolling down her cheeks, unable to be stopped, she shoved it into the lock. It clicked and fell open.

With a stifled cry, she started to get up, but the rapid staccato of her stepmère's footsteps came toward the kitchen.

Unable to gasp, she gave in to the bolt of fear without thinking and slammed it closed. She stared down at it in dismay. What had she done?

She'd just locked herself *in*?

As if seeing her situation for the first time, clearly, she

157

realized no one was coming for her. To rescue her. She had to stop wishing and hoping to be heaved onto a warrior's mount and whisked away. If she wanted to escape, then she had to climb to her feet and make it happen.

Just as Rose had done.

So she made a promise to herself. If she got another chance to escape, she was taking it.

And she wasn't coming back.

She owed these people nothing, and she would do whatever it took to find Rose on her own. Without Gautier's help.

And in spite of whatever promise she'd made to her père.

Not giving herself time to second-guess herself, she unlocked it once more, hid the key, and threw her skirt over the open manacle as her stepmère entered the room.

At the sight of her, Cosette cringed away. She couldn't help it.

Her jaw ached where the straps to her muzzle were pulled tight. Too tight.

Her stepmère towered over her, her laughter a low rumble.

Cosette's heart dropped. This couldn't be good.

"Enjoy your last moments here, girl. Once my girls get back, your services will no longer be required."

She wanted to laugh. They wouldn't survive without Cosette there to do everything for them.

Although, they had been keeping her locked up longer and longer, having her do less and less . . .

Then the rest of what she'd said caught up. Her eyes widened. Were her stepsisters . . . seeking out her fairy godmère? Now?

"And even better? Gautier is coming to propose to one of my girls tonight. He told me so himself. And I'll not have you underfoot, trying to capture his attention." The Comtesse laughed again, but this time it had a hard edge to it. "I cannot wait to be rid of you, you piece of tra—"

Cosette bolted to her feet and out the door, right past her stepmère.

"What are you—how did you—get back here this instant!"

She kept running.

"There's nowhere you can hide!" she called after Cosette's retreating form. "I'll have one of Gautier's soldiers after you, and can you imagine what he'll do once I show him the jewels you stole from me?"

Cosette didn't pause, didn't bother to reply. She simply ran for all she was worth.

Which, according to her stepmère, wasn't much.

Right until she slammed into the property line and fell back, a sizzle of pain hissing over her entire body.

As she arched her back and waited for the agony to release her, her père's voice came to her on the breeze.

Listen to your step —

"I said I would listen, not obey!" Cosette blurted out, past the muzzle.

The pain instantly ceased.

Her voice came out garbled, muffled—but loud enough that the sound echoed into the trees, meeting those of her père's.

The metal lattice covered her face, clenched her jaw tight, but she could just barely move her lips, just barely get words to form.

Yet she had to spit out three pearls before she choked on them.

She didn't know how, but she could feel the voice, waiting to finish, her promise hovering close behind.

To seal her in and trap her.

"Non," Cosette said firmly, shaking her head as she warmed to the idea.

She hauled herself to her feet and faced the boundary.

Her head spun with the fact that she could leave anytime

she was intending to come back—just not when she was trying to run away. And her père had specifically said to *listen* to her stepmère, not that she had to *obey* her.

She had no one to tell her if she was right, so she clung to that idea with her fingertips.

"I will listen to her, of course I will. But I never promised to obey." She clamped her jaw shut. Trying to speak past the muzzle was painful.

The voice tried again. *Stay here—*

"Who said I wasn't coming back?" she demanded defiantly, before the words had fully formed. "I'm just going to the well."

Another pause.

The petals stuck to the cage, and she kept having to pause between words to spit out jewels and pearls.

Thank goodness there weren't any huge ones.

Cosette started to sweat. Her stepmère could be moments behind her. Unless she'd gone for help.

Then there would be soldiers and dogs.

Surely her stepmère wouldn't risk it. Gautier would have questions if she sent his soldiers after a mere servant girl, wouldn't he? Surely she wouldn't want to risk her daughters' futures.

As if released, her père's echoey words wisped away, though her promise seemed to hold a warning for her if she didn't come back.

She fisted her hands. She was going to find a way around this curse if it killed her.

Hesitantly, afraid of the pain, Cosette poked a toe over the boundary line.

It was as if the line no longer existed.

Cosette took off into the trees.

o matter that Cosette ran swiftly, that she burst through the forest with all she had, she was still too late.

Her stepsisters stood next to the well, dressed in rags—her old rags, used for little more than cleaning—bickering as they always did.

Cosette started to move forward, to get the girls' attention, when the rumbling of a carriage met her ears. She slid down into the undergrowth, hoping she was hidden enough with the blackened foliage mostly fallen away.

The most ornate carriage Cosette had ever seen in her life—even finer than the king's, before the curse fell—rumbled into the little clearing next to the well, the overgrown path not hindering it in the slightest.

One Cosette knew well, having ridden it to the ball the past three nights, even if it was more spectacular now.

"Halt!" someone commanded from within.

The man in exquisite livery pulled on the reins, and the four pure-white horses tossed their heads and came to a begrudging halt.

The carriage door opened, and a long, delicate arm with tapered fingers, neat nails free of dirt, and mounds of lace at the elbow came out of the carriage and waited.

The man riding on the back of the carriage almost killed himself trying to get to the woman within immediately. He took her hand, and one bejeweled foot emerged from the carriage.

Cosette could only stare in wonder at the ornate shoe, encrusted with more gems than could possibly be decent, followed by blinding-white stockings, only a peek before layers upon layers of lace with an overlay of gold cloth—real gold, woven into cloth—emerged from the carriage slowly, as if the woman knew she was putting on a show and wanted to preen to the fullest for the two dumb country girls by the well, staring with their jaws dropped to their chests.

Then came a towering white wig, a single curl upon the woman's neck, face powder that turned her as milky-white as her horses, painted red lips, and a beauty mark in the shape of a heart upon her cheek, one Cosette could see clearly from her hiding spot.

No one could miss the beauty mark, which was surely the woman's intention.

The slender young woman emerged fully and stood on the stoop long enough for the girls to look their fill, as if she knew the effect she had on others and it was her due.

No matter how hard she stared, Cosette would've sworn she'd never seen this woman before in her life. But that was her fairy godmère's carriage, was it not?

Had another of the fey borrowed it?

"You there," the young woman's purring, sultry voice demanded, "peasants. Get me a drink."

Druce immediately scowled, and Stasie echoed in a dazed voice, "A drink?"

A third man ran around the carriage and draped a heavy red velvet cloth on the ground in front of the carriage, rolling it toward the well.

Even the servants looked completely different than those who'd ferried Cosette to the ball.

"Yes, yes." The woman stepped down and walked along the cloth, still holding the second man's fingertips for balance. "From the well there. Just beyond you. I thirst." She raised a perfect eyebrow. "Your well water is drinkable, I take it?"

Druce's face was a thundercloud. She propped her hands on her hips. "Your servants can get you water. Or better yet, get it yourself."

Stasie looked between them, as if she didn't know the right thing to do. Or say. "You are welcome to our well, but we are waiting for someone else."

The woman's eyebrows switched places. "More important than moi? I think not, ma chérie. Get me the water, now."

All the servants around her got nervous looks to their faces, exchanging glances. Those out of her sight, of course. The one at her side remained frozen like a statue.

Anyone else, Cosette included, could have seen that something was drastically wrong. That this woman was not to be crossed.

But Cosette's two clueless stepsisters became more entrenched in their belief that the woman could get her own water, Stasie following Druce's lead, as she always did.

"And I think you can take your hoity-toity self back to wherever you came from," Druce insisted. "No need to flaunt how much better you think you are than the rest of us."

The woman's gaze shifted to Stasie. "And you? Do you share your sister's opinion?"

Stasie bit her lip and looked between them. "Um . . ." Druce scowled harder, and Stasie wilted under her sister's glare. "You are, of course, welcome to our water. Mais oui, my sister is right. We are waiting on someone else?"

The woman didn't reply. Her face didn't change expression. The servants barely dared to breathe, let alone move.

Stasie looked more scared as the seconds ticked by, even as her sister grew more defiant, even daring to cross her arms and jut out her chin.

"So be it."

As they watched, the clouds seemed to dim and thicken, turning afternoon light into dusk in a few seconds.

The servants moved as one and disappeared behind the carriage, pinning the two girls alone under their mistress's stare.

"For your cruelty, for only thinking of yourselves, your mouths will reflect your heart. For every word spoken, the depths of your soul will crawl out, be it serpent, slug, or spider, and all will know of the poison within."

As she turned, instantly the second servant was at her side, and she walked away, once again barely holding his fingertips, leaving three dumbstruck girls in her wake.

One hidden, of course.

The third servant rolled up the red velvet runner, and the driver went from holding the horses to climbing into his seat, ready at one word from his mistress.

Just as the woman placed one shoe upon the footrest, she turned her head just enough to pin Cosette with a single glance. Her eyes narrowed when she saw the muzzle on Cosette's face. Then fury such as she'd never seen, not even on her stepmère's face, entered her eyes, and she made a snapping motion with her fingers.

With a poof, it was gone.

Cosette blinked, once again echoing her sister's go-to reaction, hardly daring to believe she was free of the accursed thing. Then the woman was inside her carriage, and it left at the same speed with which it had come.

Lifting a trembling hand to her face, Cosette pressed light fingers against the skin there, raw and sensitive to the touch, but unfettered. She choked on a sob.

Then her eyes riveted on her stepsisters.

They stood there, stunned, staring after the disappearing carriage.

And Cosette hadn't acted, hadn't done anything. Not a blasted thing.

The clearing settled into an uneasy silence in which Cosette debated revealing herself or not, since the deed was already done.

"Was that who I think it was?" Druce asked, and then Stasie screamed.

For out of Druce's mouth tumbled an enormous spider that hit the rotting leaves with a splat and skittered into the woods.

Druce's screams followed Stasie's, the girls feeding off each other as their screams grew in volume and hysteria.

"What is happening? I don't understand! What is happening?" Stasie wailed, then started gagging. Something bulged in her mouth, and Stasie clamped her hands over it, holding whatever it was in with all her might.

"Spit it out!" Druce cried. "Whatever it is, spit it out! You don't want it . . . in . . . there . . ." Druce turned and vomited, three large slugs splatting out of her mouth onto the ground.

Stasie screamed, and what was perhaps the world's longest snake slid out of her mouth onto the ground, finally slipping free of her lips once its head touched the rotten foliage.

Leaving the bucket where it lay, Druce took off for home, her face positively green, while Stasie wailed and sobbed and stumbled after her, looking intoxicated with all her weaving and tripping.

Cosette started after them, then glanced back at the well. The bucket lay next to it, in a muddy puddle, while the well covering was propped against its edge.

If anything fell in . . . if their source of water were contaminated . . .

Cosette hurried to the well, scraped most of the mud away with bark, cleaned off the bucket as best she could with her apron, and wished she had water to pour over it, then she carefully replaced the lid and left the bucket on top, in case it rained.

She glanced around the clearing. "Are you here? Please?"

A shower of petals fell at her feet, white, purple, and pink.

No answer.

"Is there anything I can do to help them? Anything at all?"

Again, more petals fell, and a single diamond.

Cosette stared at it, unsure of what to do. She couldn't lie —she'd never been able to, even as a child—so if her stepmère asked if she'd hidden any of the jewels . . .

She'd have to figure out a way to deflect. To word it in such a way that it wouldn't be a lie.

Or she simply would no longer answer.

With that thought, she dove for the jewel, pried away the loose brick at the back of the well, and hid it deep within, reminded of the fairy's words that she would one day have need of it.

Then she took off after her sisters, hoping she could help them. Hoping it wasn't permanent. Hoping her inaction wouldn't have lasting consequences.

Hoping her stepmère didn't have another muzzle hidden somewhere about her person.

I JUST WANT A FAMILY

The girls were in hysterics by the time Cosette tore into the room.

Madame Béatrice was trying unsuccessfully to calm the raging storm.

"Calm down, girls. Calm down! I can't understand a thing you're saying!"

For all her apparent poise, their mother's lofty veneer was starting to crack. Mainly making itself known by the wild look to her eyes.

And just like with Cosette, when her stepsisters cried or made noise, nothing fell out of their mouths, not even with all the unintelligible jabbering they were doing.

Then Druce's eyes fell on Cosette. "You!"

Hands straight in front of her, she flew at Cosette, intent on wrapping her hands around Cosette's throat. Cosette tucked into a ball and dropped, her arms clamped over her head, trying to protect herself.

Goodness knew no one else in the room would.

So Druce started kicking and hitting, screaming all the while.

"What"—Madame Béatrice's cold voice cut through the noise like a knife—"is that?"

Druce froze and stared in horror at what her mother was looking at. Cosette peeked out from under her arms. Stasie was still in the corner, sobbing.

A snake slithered across the floor from where Druce had been standing, and while they all watched, it tasted the air with its tongue, then curled up in a neat little coil in front of the fire, giving off an air of pure contentment.

"Cosette can tell you! It's all her fault!" Realizing what she'd done, Stasie clamped her hands over her mouth, but her mouth filled, and she bent over and spewed out another hairy, size-of-a-mop spider.

Stasie's eyes rolled up in her head and she fainted—directly onto the fainting couch at her side, Cosette couldn't help but note, not on the floor with the spider.

Her stepmère jumped up onto a three-prong footrest, nearly falling headlong into the fire—near the happily content snake—but righting herself just before she set them all free of herself.

Unfortunately.

Cosette instantly repented of the thought. As much as she wished to be free of her stepmère, she'd never wish such a gruesome death on anyone. Not even her.

The Comtesse's eyes riveted on Cosette's mouth, the mouth free of its ungodly bondage. Her lips pressed tight.

"Explain. Now." The words held tightly controlled fury, the self-control unusual for the spiteful woman.

Cosette blurted, "I tried to stop them, but it was too late. Anyone without a kind heart, a pure soul, will have coming out of their mouth exactly what's inside of them. At least, that's how it seems to work." She lowered her voice, echoing her thoughts from earlier. "I wouldn't wish such consequences on anyone."

She met Stasie's eyes—which immediately closed as her

head fell back on the couch—then Druce's in turn. Druce had a scowl on her face, but she almost looked like she was starting to believe her. With a hint of things like regret and shame.

If only that were true.

That wasn't up to Cosette. She'd always told the truth, been true to herself, and tried to help them—now it was up to them to change their actions.

Then she slowly, slowly, met her stepmère's eyes. "Your daughter's deeds came back on them. As will yours, if you're not careful."

Madame Béatrice went white with rage. "You dare threaten me? In my own home? Me, who took you in when your father abandoned you here?"

With the rest of us, her stepmère did not say, but Cosette could feel the words echo in the room as if she'd spoken them aloud.

Tears filled Cosette's eyes, and she leaned her head back, weary. "Non. Never. I warn you, because I see the path you're taking, and I do not wish it for you, for your daughters. The destruction wrought by your own hands is taking your life away, and you're letting it. Your cruelness will only grow until it consumes you, if it hasn't already."

The room was eerily quiet, Stasie not even bothering to pretend to be asleep now.

Cosette closed her eyes and kept speaking, letting her heart flow out in words. "You're right. My father left me here. He left all of us here. And whether you like it or not, we're a family now."

She didn't bother to stop the tears streaming down her cheeks, even knowing her stepsisters saw. Saw, and probably judged her for it.

"So let's be a family. Watch each other's backs. Look out for each other. Defend each other. Build each other—and this home—into something we're happy to be a part of. It can be done! We just have to work *together*."

Her eyes went to her stepmère and stayed there.

"But you have to stop treating us as you have been. We can love you, we *want* to love you, but only if you start letting us. If you stop turning us against each other and yourself." She held her stepmère's eyes, which were wide and a little crazed looking. She pressed on anyway. "You have to stop hurting us. You're *going* to stop hurting us."

No one said anything. Druce, Stasie, Madame Béatrice all were frozen, staring at her as if they'd never seen her before.

"And if she doesn't?" Stase asked quietly, something very much like hope in her voice.

The Comtesse's head whipped toward her daughter.

Grabbing a decorative bowl nearby, Stase spit out a slug with a grimace, not taking her eyes off Cosette.

"Then we're leaving," Cosette said firmly. "No one should be treated as we are. We won't let her hurt us, not ever again."

Druce burst into tears. Loud, wailing sobs.

Stasie sighed as if the weight of the world had just been rolled from her shoulders.

And Madame Béatrice stared at them all as if she couldn't believe what just happened.

The fire crackled as silent tears tracked down Cosette's face, as she cried for everything she'd lost, for everything these women refused to do for each other and themselves, and prayed with every inch of her soul that one of them would listen.

That they would *all* listen.

"I—perhaps I have—" But the Comtesse couldn't seem to get anything else out.

Her girls waited expectantly. So did Cosette, if she were being honest.

"What happened to your gift?" her stepmère demanded after a long pause.

Cosette blinked. "What?"

"Your gift. The gems. The pearls. The *diamonds*?" Her stepmère sounded panicked in a whole new way.

Cosette glanced at her lap. There were no gems, no flowers, no pearls. Nothing.

She smiled at her stepmère. "Perhaps you needed to hear my words without distractions."

Though kindly said, Cosette felt their loss. She'd only been able to hide away the one gem.

Had it happened when the fairy saw her muzzle? Saw for herself what her gift had cost Cosette, what Cosette had been unable to say? Gifting her one final diamond before ensuring her stepfamily received no more?

Her stepmère eyed her speculatively, then looked at the spider and snake and sighed.

"Girls, get these . . . creatures . . . out of here. Gautier will be here any moment, and we can't have him knowing what you've become."

Her look for Cosette held accusation, but it wasn't as . . . volatile . . . as before. More resigned.

The girls stared at their mother, stricken, whether from her words or the fact Gautier would be calling on them, Cosette couldn't tell. But one question was on all their minds: What would they do?

"We'll figure something out," Madame Béatrice said, all the fight gone from her voice. Then a wry smile touched her lips. "Together."

Though it wasn't kind, it wasn't unkind, and both girls perked up. Hope, traitorous feeling that it was, trickled into Cosette as well, and she felt her whole soul lighten.

Maybe some of what she'd said had found its mark.

But she'd seen her stepmère pretend to be kind before, and she was good at it.

Cosette was too wrung out to try to figure it out, so she

climbed to her feet, grabbed a broom and dustpan from the pantry, and came back for the snake and spider.

Druce had a vase over the spider, holding it down firmly, and the other two stood far away from the snake.

Cosette eyed him for the best way to put him outside, then slid the dustpan underneath, careful not to hurt him, and held the broom against it so he could twine up the handle if he so wished.

Then she ran outside and placed him gently in the woods, hopefully far enough away from their home that he didn't feel the need for a return visit.

Then she went back for the spider and slug.

As she was sliding the dustpan under the vase, a carriage crushed the shells in their driveway.

"Hurry!" her stepmère hissed at Cosette. Then, "Girls, go change now"—since they were still in Cosette's rags—"but remember, not a word. Oh! Fans. Hide behind your fans!"

Her stepsisters bolted up the stairs while Cosette ran outside as Madame Béatrice invited Gautier and his manservant inside and announced her girls would be down shortly.

Cosette hurried back, staring down at her worn dress and fretting over it. If she'd saved more than one jewel, just one, she would've been able to hide away a new dress too. A real dress.

But no, she had to see Gautier looking like this.

She sighed. It couldn't be helped. And hopefully, he wouldn't mind. With his own position as the king's steward, he quite possibly wasn't the kind of person to be blinded by station, but she really didn't know. She'd hoped to meet him while decked out in a ballgown.

But meeting him as herself would have to do.

"And these are my girls, Drucelle and Anastasie. Aren't they just lovely? I assure you they are twins, though they look nothing alike."

Cosette stopped right outside the servant's entrance to the room, mortified on their behalf.

If Madame Béatrice ever put in true effort to change, she most certainly had a long way to go.

Eyeing the direct path to the kitchen, wishing to disappear yet knowing this was her last opportunity, she'd just about worked up the courage to move forward when Gautier said, "But where is Mademoiselle Cosette?"

She froze mid-step, eyes wide. He knew her name?

But that could only mean—

"Cosette? How—" Her stepmère recovered quickly. "Oh, Cosette couldn't be here," she replied, in that airy way she had when trying to make people think she was nicer than she was. "I'm afraid she's returned to her family home in the country, something about being previously engaged—soon-to-be married, you understand."

Madame Béatrice's back was to the door, and she frantically waved Cosette away with one hand.

Cosette's jaw tightened. Her stepmère wasn't getting away with it. Not this time.

She took one step forward and opened her mouth to announce her presence, that she needed a word with him, when a hand clamped over her mouth, an arm snaked around her waist, and a burly man smelling of garlic and body odor and all things vile hauled her backward and down into the kitchen.

Cosette tried to scream, she tried to fight, but she was no match against the man's strength or the pressure he put on her neck. She started seeing spots, as though she might pass out at any moment.

That could *not* happen.

She clamped down on his arm with both hands and twisted, like when she gave her brothers rugburn for trying to manhandle her, and the hulking man yelped and dropped her.

For just a second, she could've sworn his arm glowed with heat, but that didn't make sense.

Cosette filled her lungs to scream, but he was back, and another besides, and they quickly tied a putrid cloth around her mouth, trussed her up, and shoved her head into a burlap sack.

"What was that?" Gautier asked as his footsteps moved toward her.

Her stepmère's lighter, heeled footsteps rushed to block his way. "I assure you, my servants are not your concern. Please, let them go about their work."

"Very well."

The men took their cue to hoist her onto their shoulders and shuffle her out of the house, fast.

Cosette writhed and made as much noise as possible, but they held her firm, and she wasn't loud enough for anyone inside the house to hear.

They'd tied the gag so firmly around her mouth, her jaw ached. In a different way than the muzzle.

Dieu, if the old woman ever gave her another wish, it would be to never have anything else tied around her mouth for as long as she lived.

She fought, but what could she do? Her body was slight, her power had always come from her kindness, while Ro always strove for physical strength, and based on what she'd just heard, her stepmere had set this up well ahead of time.

Apparently her impassioned words had come far too late.

The Comtesse had planned to get rid of Cosette as soon as her daughters came back spewing jewels—to keep her from distracting Gautier.

But he'd asked for her—why?

And now she may never know.

Cosette choked on a sob, wondering if the tears would ever stop, if she'd spend the rest of her life mourning.

Please, Rosette, where are you? I need you! her mind screamed.

But Rose didn't come riding into the clearing in a blaze of glory, arrows flying, and there was no answer to her pleas.

After carrying her well away from the house, her captors placed her on a pile of old blankets—thankfully the burlap sack over her head smelled no worse than musty oats—and a wagon pulled away from the only home left to her.

To an unknown future.

Cosette sucked in a breath as they left the property—but there was no pain, no sizzle. Apparently being taken without her consent didn't apply to whatever weird rules held her here.

Silent tears trickled down Cosette's face as the wagon bumped down the road.

38

GAUTIER TO THE RESCUE

Somehow, she'd fallen asleep. She was ashamed of herself the moment she was hauled out of the wagon, which was what woke her. What would Rose say when she found out how easily Cosette had allowed herself to be captured? *If* she ever found out . . .

After being marched down a long, cool hallway, she was shoved to her knees as one of her captors said, "We brung her, Monsieur Gautier."

The burlap sack was whipped away from her head—to a familiar smiling face.

"There she is!" he said happily.

But—it couldn't be. The odorous man had just called him Gautier, but . . . he wore the red frock coat and had danced with her every evening at the ball.

The man . . . Gautier . . . they were the same person.

Cosette felt a thousand times the fool. How had she not known? How had she not guessed? How had she not *seen*?

Stasie had tried to tell her, even.

She stared at him, eyes wide, heart pounding; he stared back, a look of delight upon his face. It took a moment, but the grin slid off his face.

"Tears?"

He traced what had to be a dirty trail down her cheek before spinning on the two other men.

"Didn't you tell her where you were taking her?"

Nervous shuffling. "Well, uh, you sees, Monsieur, you dinna tell us to say anything. We just brung her here, like you said."

"Imbeciles!" He started tugging at Cosette's gag. "Knife, now!"

Both men fumbled to obey, and within seconds, Gautier sliced the tight cloth free.

Cosette could only stare at him. Her brain had completely shut down.

He traced the lines on her face where the gag had been, then spoke in a low, dangerous voice. "If you do not leave my sight, right now, you will not walk out of this room alive."

Cosette jolted, then realized belatedly that he wasn't speaking to her.

The men headed straight for the door, but one paused. "What about our gold?"

Gautier lifted cold, dangerous eyes to the man and said nothing.

He shuffled in place a moment before apparently deciding his life was worth more than payment. The men hurried out.

Gautier struggled a moment, then closed his eyes and swiped a hand down his face. Cosette recoiled from him in fear, that look in his eyes scaring her, perhaps more than being grabbed. She wasn't certain.

She was so confused.

He muttered, "That's what I get for hiring common laborers instead of waiting for some real help."

Cosette hadn't detangled his words before he took a deep breath, dropped his hand, and smiled at her.

"Forgive me for your rough treatment, Mademoiselle. I heard of your predicament mere moments before traveling to your estate, and had to act. Had I known . . . I never would have dreamed . . ." He sighed. "Je suis désolé. I am sorry."

Cosette cleared her throat twice before being able to speak. "I assure you, no harm done, Monsieur, but I would love an explanation?"

He gently helped her off the floor and into a deeply cushioned seat. "I am at your disposal, ma belle Mademoiselle. Ask anything, and I shall endeavor to answer it."

He then poured and offered her a cup of café. She held up a hand to refuse. "Just water, s'il vous plaît."

He hastily sent a servant to fetch her some.

In that time, she found exactly what she wanted to say.

"You knew. You *knew* I was looking for you all this time, to meet you, and you didn't tell me?" She couldn't help the reproach in her tone.

To her extreme satisfaction, he looked chagrined. "Ah, but you see, my Mademoiselle, moving through the crowds in disguise was the only way I could, in fact, enjoy any moment of the fête itself. Especially a moment with you." He kissed her hand.

She couldn't hold back the words a second longer. "But my sister—I must find my sister! Please, where is she? Where has she gone? I have not heard from her in over a year . . . !"

She'd crept forward, clinging to his hands, seconds away from throwing herself at him until he gave her the precious knowledge she sought.

She couldn't hold back the desperation in every line of her face, her voice, her posture. She needed to find Rose and she needed to find her *now*.

"Ah, in that I never misspoke." He set her back from him, looking truly regretful. "You see, Mademoiselle Cosette, I do not know. I sent her for a job not long after the time of which you speak, and I, too, have not heard from her since. Je suis désolé, truly."

Cosette choked on a sob and buried her face in her hands.

"Is nothing being done to find her?" She peeked up at him through her fingers.

"Well . . ." Gautier rubbed the back of his neck. "But of course there is. I've sent many huntsmen to her last known location, but not one of them has brought back any news of her. I would like my huntress back too."

She dropped her hands. "What was the job?"

He smiled as if he were trying to let her down gently. "That I cannot say, ma belle Mademoiselle, to my deep regret. Many of her hunts were . . . most secretive. Surely you understand?"

Cosette sighed and slumped, dejected. "I suppose I do, Monsieur."

Rosette had said as much herself.

"I promise the moment I hear from her, I will contact you. I give you my word of honor."

After giving him a tremulous smile, Cosette then looked around the room. "How did I end up here? Instead of, well, wherever I was being . . . taken?"

His face darkened. "I assure you, Madame Reynard will be stripped of rank, tried for treason against the crown, and executed for what she has done to you."

A hand fluttered to Cosette's throat. "Oh, please, not that, I beg of you! She did not mean it . . ." The excuse felt paltry on Cosette's tongue.

His look said he believed her words as much as she did. "But she must be punished, oui? Had they not come to me for a higher price, had I not asked for word of you, the mysterious girl who left her glass slipper in my hosts' garden"—he brought her hand to his lips and kissed her knuckles—"I would never have known of your disappearance. Surely someone who devises such a scheme deserves what they get?"

Cosette shook her head. "Leave her fate to me, I beg of you. I would like this to remain . . . in the family."

When he didn't seem to be convinced, she fluttered her

eyelashes and widened her eyes innocently, knowing Rosette would roll her eyes and demand she speak plainly instead of trying to manipulate.

But Rose wasn't here right now, and Cosette only knew one way to get what she wanted from the masculine sex.

"Please, Monsieur Gautier. I don't think she will try anything like this again. Not after I speak to her. Not after her plan for me has been foiled and she has been found out."

"Then speak to her as my wife. Surely no harm will befall you if you have my protection."

Cosette's eyes widened, and she gasped.

Carefully, he gathered her hands in his once more. "Surely you have guessed that *you* are the Mademoiselle? The only Mademoiselle for me. I would have no other, not after you have enchanted me, body and soul."

She couldn't form a response, all thoughts of flirting thrown to the ether.

"That when I spoke of choosing a bride, that I only ever could choose you. None but you."

Truly? After he'd seen her in rags and how her stepfamily treated her?

He kissed her hands, turning them over to kiss her palms as well. Her scratched, calloused, work-weathered palms.

Gently, he withdrew her lost slipper from a satchel beside him, pulled off her work boot—she flushed that he would see her feet in such a grimy state—and slipped on the shoe with all the gentleness of a lover.

It fit like heaven.

If only she hadn't shattered the other. Perhaps whatever was on the inside would hold it together?

She pulled it from her pocket and set it gently next to the other.

As soon as they were next to each other, the cracks seemed to flee from the broken shoe, until the second shoe was just as whole as the first.

"Incroyable," Gautier breathed out. He looked up at her eagerly. "Fey made?"

Her eyes widened, and she nodded. "You know of such things?"

He chuckled. "There are a great deal of mysteries I have discovered ruling a cursed nation."

Of course. She smiled and stared at the two shoes, now whole, restored to each other. She was just slipping on the second glass slipper when Gautier spoke again.

"Won't you consider becoming my wife?"

Cosette could only gape at him, shoes forgotten.

His voice took on a teasing note. "I did pay a pretty sum to have you delivered here instead of only Dieu knows where those men were taking you."

She flushed, uncomfortable with owing him something that could never be repaid. "Of course I can never forget your kindness, Monsieur, but please, my sister . . ."

He stiffened.

Cosette continued gently. "I must find her. If you do not know where she has gone, then I must discover it." She shrugged delicately. "But who knows? After I find her . . ."

She let the words hover in the air, pregnant with expectancy.

She couldn't give him her word, couldn't promise him her hand—she knew better than that—but she couldn't deny how tempting it was to be taken away from that awful house. To be taken care of.

To be the first to learn of Rosette's whereabouts.

At that thought, it was all she could do not to blurt "Oui!" and throw herself in his arms.

She may not feel the wild stirrings, the undeniable attraction as in so many of Rosette's precious books, but surely such love came rarely, to a select few.

The safety he offered was far more tempting than being swept away.

But first . . . Rose.

He looked down, thinking over her words. Then, "Are you sure you will not reconsider? I could free you from this life at this very moment. In a heartbeat. No one need ever treat you in such a way again."

Cosette laughed, not in a cruel way. "I have never been tempted more, Monsieur, but I am not ready. I beg of you to understand. When I find my sister, when my home is in order —ask me then." She shrugged one delicate shoulder. "If you still want to, of course."

He kissed her fingertips and grinned in such a way that wasn't altogether unpleasant. "Oh, I intend to."

Cosette blushed and gave him a gentle bat of her eyelashes. "I look forward to that day."

Gautier kissed her hand again, then her wrist, then started up her arm.

And the door burst open.

"Unhand her, you brute!" Drucelle demanded.

"Yeah, leave our sister alone!" Stasie agreed.

Cosette and Gautier stared at the two girls in shock, brought up short by two guards holding them just within the threshold.

Though Gautier stared more at the snake and the spider that spewed from the girls' mouths at their outburst.

"Deepest apologies, Monsieur Gautier, but they was sneaking in, and before we knew it, they was at yer door and barging in like two little—"

Gautier pinched the bridge of his nose. "Have I employed every idiot in the country? Go! Take them to the dungeon and hold them for questioning."

Cosette was on her feet, all three of them protesting at once (though Stasie and Druce were careful to keep their mouths shut).

Gautier raised his hands to stop the clamor. "Fine, fine! Not the dungeon. The stocks in the town square?"

"Absolutely not," Cosette said firmly.

The girls were almost in tears.

Gautier turned to Cosette. "Then what would you suggest for someone who tried to sell you?"

Cosette stared at him, stunned, not sure what to say.

In fact, all three were silent at that, until Druce burst out, "We didn't know she was being sold!"

Stasie added tearfully, "We would have never stood silently by for that. Never!"

Cosette slid her a glance, not convinced, but she caved the moment she saw the stricken look on Stasie's face. Druce looked like she was ready to tear weaponry from the wall and battle Gautier for saying such a thing.

"Of course you wouldn't, dear." She turned the full brunt of her charm on Gautier. "S'il vous plaît, can you not reward their bravery? It takes a brave soul to burst into someone's home to rescue a stolen sister."

Both Stasie and Druce seemed to swell with pride, a look she loved seeing on their faces.

Non, she couldn't leave yet. She had much more work to do at home, if only to see these confident girls blossom.

She'd have to deal with her stepmère, though.

Leaving that be was not an option.

Gautier threw his hands into the air. "Fine! I can see I'm outnumbered. And by such lovely Mesdemoiselles, too."

Both girls simpered, and Cosette smiled prettily at him.

He returned her smile. "Go, take care of your home, and I will return to mine and inquire about your sister."

"Oh, will you?" Cosette didn't even think about it—she just flung her arms around him. "Merci, a thousand times, merci!"

He returned her hug before setting her back, reluctantly, and sending orders to prepare for his departure.

He paused by her on his way out the door and spoke in a

low voice. "Will you not reconsider? I will not be able to protect you from my château—unless you come with me."

She touched his arm briefly. "I am sure. I have much to do here first. But I will consider, and I will give you an answer when I am ready."

He lingered over the kiss he placed on her hand, then he and his retinue were gone.

Cosette and her sisters hurried home, her heart pounding with what to do about her stepmère.

She was not going back in the closet, she was never being chained or muzzled ever again, and she would not allow herself to be sold, that was for certain.

"Does this mean we're leaving?" Druce asked hesitantly, as if afraid of the answer.

Stasie answered before Cosette could. "Absolutely." Then she peeked at Cosette. "Right?"

Cosette's jaw went tight. "It very well could."

At their wide-eyed looks, as if they thought she'd changed her mind, Cosette felt she had to explain.

"It seems the . . . kidnapping, I suppose, was set up well ahead of time. Before we spoke with her."

"But Maman certainly didn't do anything to stop it," Druce pointed out.

"True," conceded Cosette, "but I have to wonder if she was more concerned about her girls—about both of you— looking bad in front of Gautier. Perhaps she would have stopped it. If she had more time."

All three girls were silent for a little while, dead leaves and pebbles crunching underfoot.

"Are you sure you aren't making excuses for her?" Stase asked quietly.

Cosette opened her mouth to deny it . . . then closed it. "I —don't think so?"

"You always try to see the best in everyone, to see the way they look at things," Stasie continued, "but I think you have a blind spot where our mère is concerned."

Cosette tried to object, but Stasie kept right on talking.

"I've seen the way you look at her, Cosette. You so want her to be a mother to you, but she just . . . isn't like that. Really never has been. But it's gotten so much worse since—" Stasie bit her lip.

"Since my father left and hasn't bothered to come back?" Cosette whispered.

"Oui," Stasie said apologetically.

Tears filled Cosette's eyes, and she found she couldn't respond if she'd wanted to. She *had* wanted a new mother. Wanted it more than anything.

Wanted it enough that she'd made excuses, lied to herself —even if she couldn't lie to anyone else—and hoped again and again that the Comtesse would turn to her with a beaming smile, open her arms, and wrap Cosette in all the love she had longed for these many years.

It was time for her to wake up.

As much as it might hurt for her to do so.

"Can you forgive me. For being such a fool?" Cosette choked out. "For being so . . . blind?"

Druce and Stasie immediately came on either side of her and hugged her, the three of them stopping in the middle of the road.

"There's nothing to forgive," Stasie said.

"Yeah, we felt more sorry for you, at first, when your père brought you to live with us," Druce added helpfully. "We at least knew what she was like and how to make ourselves scarce. It didn't help that you started waiting on her hand and foot, making us look like lazy—ouch! What did I say?"

Cosette bit back a laugh at the glare on Stasie's face. Druce rubbed her side where her sister had pinched her.

"What she *meant* to say was—we're sorry. For not better preparing you. For not being better sisters."

Cosette hugged them both close. "As someone wise just said, there's nothing to forgive."

The three girls hugged and laughed wetly and rubbed noses and tears on handkerchiefs and sleeves.

"Oh my, what nice shoes!" Druce said, breaking the tension. They all laughed.

Cosette pointed a toe. "They are that, aren't they? My Fée Marraine gave them to me."

Druce's eyes were huge. "You have a Fée Marraine?"

"Oui, and I'll tell you all about her as we walk home."

She'd just leave out the part where the fairy had cursed them with snakes and slugs and spiders.

"Wait a moment!" Cosette cried. "The slugs and snakes. Where are they?"

The girls looked at each other, eyes wide.

"I'm—almost afraid to say anything," Druce said, screwing her eyes closed, then peeking at the ground. "Hey! You're right."

Stase laughed. "I've never been so happy not to have . . . those things . . . coming out of my mouth!"

"What do you think happened?" Druce asked.

Cosette beamed at them. "I think your hearts are finally reflecting how kind I knew you could be. When you came to rescue me, when you finally acted on putting someone else before yourself—I think that broke the curse. It's just a guess, of course."

Both girls looked happier than she'd seen them, well, ever.

They set off once more for the Comtesse's home.

They hadn't gone three steps before Stasie tugged them to a halt. "But we're packing our bags when we get there, oui?"

Cosette swallowed, hard. "Oui. But first—do you think we can talk to her? Just make sure . . . ?"

They were already shaking their heads.

Stasie said, "She keeps promising to change, Cosette. When we were younger, she apologized so much. Cried, even. Heartbroken, wrenching sobs. But it's gotten worse. So much worse."

"But where will we go?" Cosette asked in a small voice.

"Don't you have siblings?" Druce asked.

Cosette nodded.

Druce shrugged. "Then we'll start there. And if that doesn't work, well, maybe Gautier needs scullery maids."

Cosette flushed scarlet. She couldn't imagine walking up to Gautier and saying, "I still haven't decided if I'll marry you, but can I scrub your vegetables for a pittance in the meantime?"

She'd rather do just about anything else.

"Or, you know, you could marry him and set us up with some of his gorgeous huntsmen," Druce said, waggling her eyebrows. "You know they'll be noblemen if he ever takes the throne. Besides, I've heard his lead huntsman, Liam, is just about the most handsome man this world has ever known."

Cosette fell back a little as her stepsisters hurried ahead, speaking of the huntsmen's best features and who was most eligible—based on looks.

She couldn't help her worry. Would she even be able to leave before her père returned and released her from her promise?

39

CONSEQUENCES

The three girls hurried toward the side entrance into the kitchen when the wind stilled, and everything went quiet.

Stasie and Druce were each on one of the steps leading into the kitchen, Cosette just below them, and they turned as one to see what had prickled their senses.

There, in the clearing at the back of the house, just past the wood line, stood a tall woman. Her eyes, hair, and hands were dark, shadows writhing around her. She wore them like clothing that was constantly moving, reaching.

She clutched a long staff, its tip like a claw reaching for the heavens.

Her voice, when it came, held unimaginable fury, directed at Cosette's stepsisters. "You. I have something against you."

All three girls stood frozen, as if she held them there.

"You would dare fetter her, the kindest thing that has ever happened to you? You would *dare* take my gift to this world and treat her as you do your worst humans?" Her voice dropped, the deep timbre rattling Cosette's bones. "You would dare . . . *sell* her?"

Cosette's mouth popped open. How had she found that

out, yet not heard their conversation as they were fleeing home?

What *was* this woman? For even though she wasn't the gnarled grandmère of before, nor the blonde beauty in the woods, she was clearly the same woman.

Though Cosette wouldn't have known it by looking at her —not one of her faces resembled the other.

And she'd missed so much, misunderstood so many things —things Cosette couldn't tell her—how had she gotten this one thing right . . . at the wrong time?

The creature lifted her hands, and the shadows rose with them, trailing off her fingers like smoke that lived.

"I should have made your throats burst with every spider you spewed from the depths of your soul! I should have left your empty husks on the forest floor instead of giving you yet another chance, for *her* sake."

Cosette tried to make peace. "S'il vous plaît, Fée Marraine, that is not necessary, I assure you—"

"Enough!" The vengeful fairy turned on Cosette next. "Where do I even begin with you? First of all, you did not heed my warning and return before sunrise. I've never met a mortal who has survived sunrise, chère. You are lucky indeed, and that is all I can say on the matter. Second, you said you wanted to go to the ball to dance with your friends, not woo a suitor into proposing!"

Cosette's mouth fell open. "I said no such thing! Do not put words in my mouth, Madame."

The fairy did not like that; her jaw tightened accordingly. What kind of godmother had Cosette's mère found for her? Or was her story even a little true?

"Monsieur Gautier does not suit. You will not pursue him."

A little rebellion roiled up in Cosette's stomach. The one thing she and her sister had in common—neither responded well to ultimatums. "I shall take your wishes under advisement."

"See that you do. You will not like what happens if you do not." The fairy godmère turned away. "And you!"

Suddenly Cosette's stepmère was there, eyes wide, hands shaking, a wet spot growing on her dress.

One hand stretched toward the stepsisters, her staff pointed at Madame Béatrice, the fairy seemed to hold them in place, even though she stood all the way across the clearing.

"How would you like to know how it feels to be *muzzled*?"

Even as she spoke the words, skin started to grow from the corners of the Comtesse's mouth, making the O of her lips smaller and smaller until . . . there was no mouth.

Her stepmère started screaming, the sound muffled, only coming from her throat.

Cosette's hands flew to her face and she held in her own scream as best she could, terrified that the woman's gaze would fall on her next—even if she was defending Cosette.

What Cosette had wished for, had longed for—for them to know what it felt like, for someone to defend her against them —had turned into a horror. A nightmare.

And all she wanted to do was wake up. To make it stop.

The creature's eyes whipped toward her then, but they skipped over her and landed on Druce and Stasie instead.

Cosette almost fainted from relief. Which was swiftly followed by terror for her stepsisters.

"And you two. You think your lives are hard now? I will suck them from your wretched bodies, and every day you do not thank her, praise her, *gush* over every small thing she does for you, you will be one step closer to the grave, your very bodies growing old before their time. And you will feel that agony for the rest of your pathetic lives."

Her face grew even more hard, if that were possible, as if it were chiseled from ice. "What better way to realize how much you need her than if you cannot see?"

She lifted the hand that held them into the air, then drew it down swiftly. Two crows separated from the trees, rose into the sky, and dove toward the sisters.

The girls screamed, unable to move, unable to shield themselves. The crows landed on their faces, held tight with their long claws, and started ripping and tearing their eyeballs from their sockets. One came free, which was quickly devoured, before they started on the second.

This jolted Cosette into action. She flew at the woman, her tongue loosened.

"Non, stop! Arrête!" Cosette threw out her hand and batted the woman away without touching her. She stumbled to a halt, frozen in shock, then backed away, turned, and ran to her stepsisters' sides.

They were screaming, faces raised to the sky, unable to defend themselves as the crows tore out their eyes.

Cosette choked on a sob over the bloody mess. She tried to shoo the birds away, but they wouldn't budge.

With a deep breath, Cosette seized one bird and threw it into the air. And just like that, the witch's hold snapped on the crow. It fluttered away, dazed, cawing at the world. But Cosette was already doing the same with the other.

The crows fluttered up to the roof, an eyeball with a bloody, pulpy stem trailing out of each of their beaks. They tossed back their heads and these eyeballs, too, disappeared into their gullets.

This woman was no fairy; she was a witch. She had to be.

She'd made a bargain with the kind of creature Rose spent her life hunting and defeating.

Cosette felt sick.

Stase and Druce collapsed on the steps, bloody trails down their cheeks, eye sockets hollow, faces slack.

Suddenly, Cosette could see the witch's hold on them as glowing strands of darkness.

She broke the strands off her sisters and gently helped

them sit up, cradling them close as they mewled and made the most terror-filled sounds she'd ever heard.

Rage swelled in Cosette's heart and crested over the edge. "How dare you!" She jumped to her feet and faced the fairy-witch. "I didn't ask for this. I didn't ask you to punish them!"

The witch lay where Cosette had thrown her, panting. She seemed to have aged drastically. "They deserve it. They deserve it for what they did to you. You know they do."

"I—you don't understand. You heap coals upon their head by kindness, not by tearing their eyes out!"

The old woman sneered. "And that has worked so well for you, has it?"

Cosette flushed. She couldn't argue. She didn't know how she could've made anything better, done anything differently, but she knew she didn't want this.

Clenching her fists, she spat, "Get out of here. Right now. And do not *ever* come back."

"You won't survive this without me, chère."

"I don't care," Cosette said defiantly. "I will make my own path. Choose my own way. And it won't be yours."

The witch stumbled to her feet, looking older and even more weary, and leaned heavily on her staff. "Looks like I'm going to have to save you from yourself."

In a move so fluid Cosette almost didn't see it coming, she thrust out her staff.

In response, Cosette flung out her hands, just as the witch had done, and felt the smallest fizzle of . . . something . . . at her fingertips.

The witch's shadows writhed as they tore toward all three girls and the Comtesse.

And fell at Cosette's feet.

Mouth parted, Cosette held her hands before her, holding back whatever it was the witch was trying to do to them. Holding back the writhing shadows.

A shield of some kind stood between them, a shield of

Cosette's making, though she couldn't have said how. She almost couldn't believe it was happening.

Even though she was seeing it before her very eyes.

The witch sagged as if drained, and the onslaught ceased. "Fie on you! I don't have time to coddle a spoiled princess while my own kingdom is at war. You want to live here? Continue to be abused and belittled and looked down upon when you could be . . . bah! I cannot say. Fine. Choose your own fate, dearie, and I wash my hands of you. I don't have time to deal with your little tantrum."

Cosette raised her chin, hardly able to decipher what any of that meant. "That is all I want. To make my own path."

She pointed her staff at Cosette. "Mark my words, young Mademoiselle. You will regret this moment for the rest of your life."

A swirl of smoke enveloped her, and then she was gone.

Cosette rushed back to her stepsisters and took Stasie into her arms. She looked around for her stepmère, who had apparently climbed into the bushes the moment she was released, and from the sounds of her sobs, had a mouth again.

An image Cosette hoped to block for the rest of her life.

She turned back to her stepsisters. "There, there, dear ones. Here, let me see."

Stasie's hands were held before her, shaking, like she wanted to cover her eyes but was scared to touch them. Her mouth opened and closed in wordless horror.

Cosette took in the empty socket, where the eyeball and root had been torn out, leaving bloody, gushing trails down both cheeks. Stasie was in shock, unable to make a sound, while Druce was keening and wailing so hard, Cosette was afraid she might vomit or rob herself of breath soon and pass out.

Not that either reaction was uncalled for.

Compassion welled in Cosette's heart, and with it, confidence. "Oh my darlings, let me help you."

Copying a story her mère had once told her about the Healer, she swiped up some of the dirt near their front stoop and spit in it, mixing it into a thick mud.

"There you are."

Not questioning it, not wondering how or why in all the realms these were her actions, she fitted the balls of mud to the empty eye sockets and held her hands over them.

"Be healed, dear one."

Warmth spread from her shoulders, down her arms, and into her palms. The tingling warmth poured out of her in seconds, and when she pulled her hands away, Stasie was blinking at her, the only remnant of her ordeal the bloody tear stains on her cheeks.

Cosette gave her a kind smile, kissed the backs of her hands, and moved to Drucelle.

Stasie jumped up to help prop her sister upright, eyes wide with wonder, though still dazed, still unsure how to react.

Druce was limp, arms flopping. "No. No! How could she do this? Just kill me, please. I can't live like this. I can't live like this!"

Cosette swiftly repeated the same actions, and once the warmth had left her palms, moved away.

Druce sat there, blinking at her. "What? How—? What did you do?"

She waved her hands, started to touch her eyes but jerked away before she could, then reached out and trailed her fingertips down Cosette's cheek.

Cosette smiled. "I was more than happy to help, but praise the Creator. It was His power, not mine."

Then she slapped Cosette, hard. Cosette's hand flew to her burning cheek, and Drucelle looked just as startled as the other two girls.

But then she screamed, "Witch. Witch!"

Cosette reached for her. "I'm not—it's not that . . ."

Drucelle scrambled back, cringing away from Cosette's

hand. "You had her do that to us, didn't you? Didn't you! What, to teach us one of your lessons? Non, don't touch me!"

Drucelle bolted to her feet and ran, the wild look in her eyes haunting Cosette long after she'd gone.

Cosette peeked at Stasie, who was still sitting there, staring at her.

"Are you going to run off screaming too?" Cosette couldn't help but ask.

Stasie gave a brief wry smile before she was back to studying Cosette's face as if she'd never seen her before. "Non . . . I don't think so," she said hesitantly. Then, "Merci beaucoup."

Cosette nodded with a kind smile, then eyed the woods.

Just what had the witch meant that she would regret her actions all her days?

40

A BEAUTIFUL ENDING

*L*ife settled into an uneasy rhythm after that. There was no more talk of running away, for one thing.

Drucelle couldn't stand to be in the same room as Cosette, Stasie watched her closely, as if she was just waiting for her next magic trick, and Madame Béatrice looked hollow, empty. Often staring at nothing.

But at least she'd stopped yelling at the girls.

Almost ignored them completely, in fact.

Any time she started working herself up, nitpicking or criticizing, Cosette would level a cool look her way, hand her a hoe or garden shears, and Madame Béatrice would hurry away and take out her frustrations on their garden.

It flourished under her hand.

Amazingly, all the petals Cosette had left trailing behind her grew any seed they planted with it, even in the dead soil, something they'd discovered quite by surprise.

When their trash heap exploded with thick vines and monstrous pumpkins.

Thank goodness the wagons now came this far with food and seeds besides. They were going to be all right. Maybe more than all right.

The front doors slammed open, their boom echoing through the house. "Is no one here to greet me in my own home?"

Cosette's head came up, her hands and hair covered in flour. Stasie's hands stilled from chopping vegetables, and Druce, who was as far away from Cosette as she could physically get, paused from buttering tart tins.

"Is that—?" Stase started to ask.

"Michèl-Pierre! You are home!" Madame Béatrice's warm voice came from the front of the house.

The girls dusted or wiped their hands on their aprons and hurried toward them. They piled up in the archway into the foyer.

Cosette's père stood there, rumpled, swaying slightly on his feet. "Where is my wife?" he slurred. "I was expecting a Comtesse, not a street urchin."

The girls gasped, but Madame Béatrice remained calm, primly folding her hands in front of her dirty smock.

"Would you like to see the garden? It is coming along nicely. We've already had our first harvest of—"

"I don't care about that!"

Cosette winced on her father's behalf. She'd so hoped he'd found happiness, and for a while there, he had. But now this? If he was sloshed in the middle of the day, his contentment had worn off rather quickly.

"Where are my girls?" He ambled to the marble staircase and called up them, "Cosette? Anya! Dru-druzilla!"

"Drucelle," their mère said calmly.

"That's what I said."

Cosette took a deep breath, offering her sisters apologetic looks. "Right here, Père," she said softly.

He spun on them, and a huge smile spread across his face. "There are my girls!"

Cosette couldn't make herself smile back. His wasn't a real smile, and she knew what was coming.

"Père," the other girls said dutifully, coming forward to offer him a kiss on the cheek.

"Don't touch me. Covered in—what is that? Flour? Bah! Look like servants, the lot of you."

"What news do you bring us, Papa?" Cosette asked, trying to cover for the hurt on her stepsisters' faces, trying to brace herself for what was to come.

"Pack your bags, girls. We're going on a trip!"

The floor must've heaved, because Cosette staggered, and she found herself clinging to Stasie, who was giving her an odd look.

"Ooh, what kind of trip, Papa?" Druce asked, somewhat lively for the first time since their ordeal with the crows.

"With all due respect, husband, we must stay here and protect our interests. The garden, not missing the wagon master's new route, guarding the well . . ."

"If I say we're going, then we'll be going, and make no mistake!" Père bellowed.

Cosette was too numb to wince. Not again. Oh no, not again.

Madame Béatrice breathed in deeply through her nose. "And where might that be, husband?"

"Not that I need to tell *you*, but Gautier owes me money. Or rather, your sister. And through her, me."

It took Cosette half a heartbeat to realize he'd started speaking to her. And of course he would think anything Rose earned belonged to him, disowned or not.

Especially with how quickly funds of any kind slipped through his fingers.

"'Member all that gold that came funneling through when we lived at the old house? Well, it stopped. And I dinna quite realize it till recently—quite recently, in fact—but then you know what I discovered?"

He waited for Cosette to shake her head, so she achingly obliged.

"I find out it came from Gautier. For yer sister. For her hunts."

It was the first time he had spoken of Rose without contempt—spoken of Rose at all, really. Not since that night he'd thrown her out and declared his daughter dead to him.

He stroked his patchy beard and slurred, "Not bad a'tall, if I do say so myself."

Madame Béatrice tried to wrangle the conversation back. "But surely you do not need us all to go . . ."

"If I say we're going, then we're going!" he shouted. Then he grinned, his moods fluctuating rapidly with the stench of drink seeping from his very pores. "Besides, I think it's time to reclaim your family home. Much more room there, eh?"

"But the wagon!" Stasie hissed to her mère.

They were all thinking it. The wagon master had only just been convinced to come this far, thanks to Gautier. Madame Béatrice's biggest château was much farther away, near Paris, and the journey would be dangerous. No one went to Paris. Not with the wolves that had overrun the city. How would they survive?

If only the Comtesse had known what she was getting into by marrying her père. If only she hadn't been dragged into this.

"Husband, we are staying here," Madame Béatrice said firmly.

"If I say we're going—" her père started.

"You lost this house, didn't you?" Cosette asked quietly. Her voice was like a thunderbolt. "Gambling. You lost this house, after you lost our family home, and now we must move before the new owners get here."

The silence that followed was charged with pain, with disbelief—with shame on Cosette's part.

"Is this true, husband?"

Her père stood there, hands dangling at his sides, the

expression of hopeless defeat more heartbreaking than all the blustering he'd been doing to hide it away.

"I'm right, aren't I, Papa?"

"Michèl, non! Say it is not true!" The stunned expression on Madame Béatrice's face broke Cosette's heart just a little more.

She'd been doing so well. Cosette had just figured out how to get through to her. And now this? How far back would that set—everything?

Père's shoulders slumped. "We have an hour. Pack what you can. No furniture. Nothing of value. We're leaving."

He ambled away, probably to his office to drink until it was time to leave. Probably expecting a servant to pack for him. Would they have to carry him out?

Madame Béatrice spoke into the quiet. "Girls, do as he said. Pack. Fit as much as you can into the wagon"—her eyes met Cosette's—"take what we need to survive. And perhaps some strong café for your père?"

Cosette nodded, trying to convey how sorry she was with a look.

Madame Béatrice accepted it with a tilt of her head. Then she turned, lifted her hoe, and made for the garden.

The girls rushed around the house, Drucelle crying and Stasie sniffling, stuffing clothes, cleaning supplies, and anything they could reasonably take with them into small trunks and valises.

Cosette made certain to haul her mère's trunk from the attic.

An hour! How could they do it all in an hour? And how long had their conversation with Père taken before he'd finally told them? How long had it taken him to find the château he'd only briefly visited since his marriage? They probably had far less.

Cosette didn't have much, but she took the time to help

her sisters pick out sturdy cottons instead of silks, work clothes instead of ballgowns.

From what she'd heard of Madame Béatrice's summer château in the west, a fire had gutted it, part of the roof had fallen in, and without the upkeep every château required, nature had started to worm its way in.

And travel would take much longer than in the past, with having to skirt Paris so widely.

Hoping she wouldn't take too long, she made a quick trip to the well to retrieve her one diamond, which she swiftly sewed into the hem of her best work dress.

Cosette hurried into the kitchen and stopped. There, spread all over the counters, was the remnants of their meal they'd just been so happily preparing.

She covered her mouth, that sight harder to take than any other. They had food, finally! And they'd just planted a garden. Every seed they'd planted from the wagon master, along with one of the rose petals that had fallen from Cosette's mouth, had thrived, unlike anything else in this dead soil.

And they'd planted the last of the petals. The last of the seeds. They couldn't take any of that with them. She didn't know how digging up and transplanting an entire garden would even work.

Would they be set upon on the road? Would thieves—or worse, wolves—take even their meager belongings?

And would the wagon master ever be convinced to go so far out into such dangerous areas?

"Cosette, do you know where my—oh." Stasie came to a stop behind her, surveying the wreckage.

Druce was a few steps behind, a dazed look on her face, but she still wouldn't meet Cosette's eyes.

"I am so sorry . . ." Cosette started.

"Girls."

Their heads came up to find Madame Béatrice framed in the kitchen doorway leading to the courtyard.

"I see your satchels and trunks are in the wagon. Please continue making food."

Druce looked around. "All of it?" she asked sullenly.

They were planning on preserving whatever vegetables were left over from the tarts. Now they would have no time to store them in the glass jars lining the countertops.

"All of it," she said firmly and left.

The girls fell to the work, thankful to have something to do, and after much longer than an hour had passed, a neat row of vegetable tarts, quiches, and soft, pillowy mounds of bread lined the windowsill and work tables.

Stasie sighed. "I'm going to miss this place."

She leaned against Cosette, who put her arm around her waist, as Druce came up and leaned on Stasie's other side, carefully holding herself away from Cosette's arm.

Cosette tried not to let it bother her. She'd extend her friendship whenever Druce was ready for it.

Almost like magic, Madame arrived just as the pastries were done. "Clean up and change, girls. Take the time to look presentable, please."

She stood resplendent in her burgundy travel clothes, every bit the Comtesse her position demanded.

"Cosette, please take the bread to the wagon."

The girls hurried to do as they were told, then ran through the house for another quick check. They didn't want to leave anything of use behind.

When they met at the top of the stairs, they exchanged glances, took a deep breath, and headed down together. They clutched each other's hands, Stasie in the middle.

Before they'd reached the bottom of the marble staircase, a pair of Gautier's soldiers, based on the livery they wore — just like the ones who'd chased Cosette in the garden — came into view. They were happily eating the warm tarts the girls had worked on all morning.

"And these are my daughters. Mademoiselle Drucelle,

Mademoiselle Anastasie, and Mademoiselle Cosette. They made the delicious pastries you are enjoying, Messieurs, as a thank you for coming in our greatest hour of need."

Mouths stuffed full, the soldier's eyes lit with interest. They choked down their food, brushed crumbs from their mouths and shirts, and bent over the Mesdemoiselles' hands to kiss them.

Cosette couldn't help but notice she wasn't the only one batting her eyelashes and offering coy smiles.

The soldiers were reduced to dumbstruck fools.

It was a lovely distraction after a debilitating hour.

Madame smiled. "Now that you have kindly allowed us to depart in dignity, we offer the rest of these tarts to you and your men."

One of the soldiers scrambled to take the tray from Madame.

He'd barely grasped it when Madame turned and said lightly, "Come, girls."

Cosette hurried after them, casting one last shy look at the soldiers, before tripping lightly down the steps and being handed up into their wagon by more eager soldiers. Several she'd even danced with at the ball.

And been chased by. She wouldn't forget that anytime soon.

Not that they noticed who she was in her light-blue home-spun dress.

Père sat slumped in the driver's seat, a dazed, dejected cast to his face. He took up the reins as soon as the women settled into the cart.

Before Père could flick the reins, the Comtesse laid her hand over his. "Michèl-Pierre, a moment, if you please. Might my girls and I stay with family? I have a cousin on the way, and I'm sure Cosette would be happy to see her brothers and sisters once more without our being underfoot. Then you can come for us after your business with Gautier is complete?"

Père paused, thinking.

Her voice turned warm like melting butter. "It is such a long and harrowing journey. Surely it will be much faster if you don't have *four* ladies to look after." She batted her eyelashes once.

Cosette didn't know how she felt about being left behind, with her père, who could not be trusted. On one hand, she was pleased to be away from the three women, pleased to see Gautier again. Possibly, accept his proposal?

On the other . . . it was somewhat insulting that her awful stepmère wanted away from *her*.

Then she remembered her stepmère had good reason never to want to see Gautier again.

Her père looked pleased. "Why, that's just what we'll do! My business with Gautier shouldn't take long at all. Cousins, you say? Might they be interested in a new business venture?"

He flicked the reins, and the wagon jolted forward.

The Comtesse let him prattle on, turning her attention to the road.

Some rough-looking men stood off to the side, just off their property, arms crossed and scowls fierce.

"Eyes ahead," Madame commanded just under her breath. Then, louder, "There are more tarts in the kitchen, Messieurs. Be sure to eat your fill!"

The soldiers cheered and moved away, streaming in and out of the house. Cosette couldn't help but note that the soldiers came out with more than just food.

Cosette wondered if she should say anything, but the gleam in her stepmère's eye said she already knew.

Cosette stared after the men dismantling the life she's built for herself, piece after hard-fought-for piece.

Her mind drifted back over her time here, over how many hours she'd spent daydreaming of Rose thundering through the gates, seated on her gleaming horse, whisking Cosette away to a better life.

Her dreams had not come true.

If she wanted to be free, if she wanted a different life, she would have to make it happen.

She took a deep breath. Père was going to see Gautier? Well then. Perhaps it was time to say yes.

Marriages had been built on far less.

And if anyone could help her find Rosette, it was he.

Cosette turned toward the road just as they rounded the bend and their garden came into view. She gasped.

It had been destroyed. Plants uprooted, stalks cut and lying on their sides, greenery strewn everywhere.

Cosette looked to where her stepmère was sitting on the wagon bench, and now the gleam in her eye looked closer to madness.

Cold, shaken, and despairing, Cosette wrapped her arms around herself and settled in for the long journey to Gautier's château in Reims.

Maybe a quick nap in the back of the wagon wouldn't be untoward. She'd dream of Rose and a better life.

And if Gautier proposed again? *When* he proposed? Well then, she would accept. Immediately.

Anything to make sure her family never went through this kind of humiliation ever again.

THE END

REVIEWS

Did you enjoy this book? Please leave a review!
It helps our authors more than you can possibly know.
Thank you so much!

~The L2L2 Publishing Team

AUTHOR'S NOTE
AND ACKNOWLEDGMENTS

A huge thank you to my newsletter subscribers, for whom I wrote this book!

I am so honored you allow me into your inbox, and I can't even tell you how much I love it when you respond to one of my emails. I hope you love this story!

I also want to thank Heidi, Cathrine, and Alicia for not only reading my story pre-publication, but also for giving me incredible feedback to make it stronger. Thank you for such lovely endorsements!

This started out as a tiny little short story, a sweet tale about Cosette's time with her stepmère while Ro is locked up in the beast's château, and blossomed into a much-bigger novella that was . . . not quite as sweet.

(We—as in, I—are still calling it a novella, even if it burst past 50k words and is straining the bounds of a novella.)

I always knew I would include the fairy tale "Diamonds and Toads" by Charles Perrault, but once I added the original "Cinderella" elements by the same author, both fairy tales fought for dominance.

Since I am a discovery writer, the way I outline is *after* the story is fully written, to see if there are plot holes, flat charac-ters, repetitions, or any other oopsies, and my goodness.

Both fairy tales tried to take center stage.

And wouldn't give way to the other.

The original French tales are very similar—both have evil older stepsisters and an evil stepmère. Both include abusing the youngest, the sweetest, kindest soul imaginable, and both include fairy godmother elements (attending the ball in one, gifts of precious gems falling from her mouth in the other).

Both include consequences for the stepsisters being so evil —in one, after the stepsisters cut off their own toes and heel to fit the glass slipper, birds peck out their eyeballs; in the other, they are cursed with toads and snakes falling out of their mouths for their unkindness.

And the beautiful young Mademoiselle forgives them instantly and tries to protect her unkind stepsisters, leading them to a better life through her kindness.

I absolutely loved digging in to the various elements of these tales (and the many different versions) and not only making them my own, but figuring out how to make them play well together in *The Lost Slipper*.

There are so many versions, in fact, I encourage you to find a few and see which one resonates most with you!

And I hope you enjoyed what this story of mine (and now yours!) became.

Drucelle and Anastasie won't be back for a few more books yet, but I hope when they are, they (and their mère) will have blossomed into lovely young Mesdemoiselles who can hold their heads up high and show kindness to others themselves.

Happy reading!

~Michele Israel Harper

ABOUT THE AUTHOR

Michele Israel Harper spends her days as an acquisitions editor for L2L2 Publishing and her nights spinning her own tales. Sleep? Sometimes . . .

She has her master's degree in publishing, is slightly obsessed with all things French—including Jeanne d'Arc and *La Belle et la Bête*—and loves curling up with a good book more than just about anything else.

Author of ten published novels (and more on the way), Michele prays her involvement in writing, editing, and publishing will touch many lives in the years to come.

Visit MicheleIsraelHarper.com to keep in touch or to learn more about her!

About the Author

Michele loves to hear from her readers! Follow her on social media, check out her website, or drop her a line to let her know what you thought of The Lost Slipper. *Happy reading!*

www.MicheleIsraelHarper.com
Facebook: @MicheleIsraelHarper
Twitter: @MicheleIHarper
Instagram: @Michele_Israel_Harper

Be sure to sign up for her newsletter for bookish news!
MicheleIsraelHarper.com/My-Newsletter

Beast
Hunter
A Prequel Novella to Kill the Beast
Michele Israel Harper

THE COMPLETE STORY
WISDOM & FOLLY
SISTERS
MICHELE ISRAEL HARPER

More from L2L2 Publishing

If you enjoyed this book, you may also enjoy:

Meet the world's biggest scaredy-cat, Candace Marshall. She won't watch horror movies or sleep with the lights off. Seriously. Throw in zombies and life-or-death survival alongside her favorite actor, Gavin Bailey, and things get interesting fast. She might even surprise herself with . . . courage? And just when she thinks it can't get worse than zombies, it does. Don't miss this lighthearted adventure.

WHERE WILL WE TAKE YOU NEXT?

Discover *Beast Hunter,*
Kill the Beast, Silence the Siren,
or *Quell the Nightingale*
Read *Wisdom & Folly Sisters,*
Shiver with *Ghostly Vendetta,*
and Devour *Zombie Takeover.*

All at
Love2ReadLove2WritePublishing.com/Bookstore
or your local or online retailer.

Happy Reading!

ABOUT L2L2 PUBLISHING

Love2ReadLove2Write Publishing, LLC is a small traditional press, dedicated to clean or Christian speculative fiction.

Speculative fiction includes any fantastical element, and usually falls in the genres or the many subgenres of Fantasy or Science Fiction.

We seek stunning tales masterfully told, and we strive to create an exquisite publishing experience for our authors and to produce quality fiction for our readers.

The Lost Slipper is at the heart of what we publish: a fairy tale that revisits the classics and turns them into something new that we hope will delight our readers.

All of our titles can be found or requested at your favorite online book retailer, local bookstore, or favorite local library.

Visit L2L2Publishing.com to view our submissions guidelines, find our other titles, or learn more about us.

And if you love our books, please leave a review!

~The L2L2 Publishing Team